MW00878334

AZTEC YOGA
A Novel

Kool A.D.

1. EL CERRITO NATURAL

Fausto was walking around El Cerrito, whistling a tune to himself, a jazz number. The big ol' nice hot yellow sun was up there brilliating in the 'lectric blue sky dappled with funny lil puffy clouds. There was a pleasant lil breeze rustling through the hyper green leaves of the trees, birds tweeting, and whatnot. 'Twas a sweet lil idyl.

He was in town visiting his auntie and unc and his lil newborn baby cuzzo. Tio Marty was at work and Tia Malika and prima Aylin were napping together so he figured he'd strike out on a lil paseo through the quaint lil suburban neighborhood.

He hadn't walked but a couple blocks when a beautiful amethyst-colored butterfly landed on his shoulder, said: "Sup."

"Sup, Mariposita."

"Chillin, you?"

"Chillin too, ride with me."

And she did, whispering directions into his ear, "turn left here," etc.

The butterfly choreographed a long, winding, weaving hike; up through Kensington, down through south Kensington, on into Paradise Hills, where his folks first shacked up. All the while, Fausto and Mariposita talked about whatever popped into their heads: books, movies, music, politics, philosophy, etc. Fausto was usually a dude of few words, and he had only just met Mariposita when she landed on his shoulder but the connection was so immediate and real, it was as if they had known each other forever.

They passed by the house where his uncle and aunt used to live with his mom and pop.

"My folks used to live here my my auntie and uncle," he told Mariposita.

"Nice house."

"Yeah, my folks ended up moving down south of the border to Santa Sirena, that's where they raised me."

"Never been."

"It's nice, mellow, kinda slow. There's a casino in town, and I don't mean to brag but I have supernatural luck at gambling: dice, cards, roulette, anything really but mostly dice. Been gambling since I was a kid, I moved out when I was real young, stayed mostly in hotels and motels for years, Tijuana, Las Vegas, Macau..."

"I could tell you were lucky when I landed on your shoulder, that's why I chose you in the first place."

"Chose me? For what?"

"Keep going straight another few blocks then turn left on Malcolm X, I'll show you."

He did as he was told.

A few blocks down Malcolm X, she said, "OK, here we are."

It was a small storefront, sign read:

"AZTEC YOGA"BOTANICA YOGA AZTECA(IS-LAMO-JUDAIC TECHNOLOGIES, AFRICA CHRIST SCIENCE, VELADORAS, PERFUMES, ACEITES, HECHIZOS MAGICOS, IDOLOS, POESIA YORU-BA, PAN GLOBAL SYNCRETIC PHILOSOPHIES & TACTICS WITHIN)⨂⨂⨂⨂⨂ ⨂⨂⨂⨂⨂⨂⨂⨂⨂⨂⨂⨂⨂-⨂⨂⨂⨂⨂ ⨂⨂⨂⨂⨂⨂⨂⨂⨂एज़टेक योगा इस्लामो-जुडाईक टेक्नोलॉजीज⨂⨂⨂⨂⨂⨂⨂⨂⨂⨂ ⨂⨂⨂⨂⨂⨂ ⨂⨂⨂⨂⨂⨂⨂⨂ ⨂⨂⨂⨂ ⨂⨂⨂⨂⨂非洲基督教科学 合作哲学和战术

He'd been down this street more than a few times but for whatever reason had never noticed this lil botanica. It didn't look new. On the contrary it looked at least a hundred years old.

They went inside.

The brujita behind the counter lit up when they walked in: "Mariposita! Mucho tiempo sin verte, como andas."

"¿Bien, bien, como esta usted, Ife?"

"¿Bien, bien, y quien es tu novio?"

"Fausto."

"Hola, mucho gusto."

"Mucho gusto."

Ife took Fausto and Mariposa into an electric blue room in the back, completely empty save for one pink glowing orb of light.

"¿Que es eso?" Fausto asked.

"¡LA MAGIA!!" said Mariposita and Ife in unison.

"¿Y que hace?

"Todo."

"Wow."

On their way out, Ife gave Fausto a smoothly polished pink pebble about the size of a standard issue marble: "Cuidala."

"¿Que es?"

"Tu lo descubrirás."

"OK."

They continued on their walk, conversing with the intimacy of long time lovers.

"Where to now?" asked Fausto.

"You'll see."

They walked to the end of Malcolm X, then walked the length of Martin Luther King Jr. Way, then they walked the length of San Pablo, then they walked the the length of Azteca and at the end of that long and winding avenue they found a pyramid, climbed to the top. At the top was an opening.

"Jump in," said Mariposita.

"What about you?"

"I'll wait outside."

Fausto shrugged and leapt.

2. CANTOS

Fausto fell for a hundred years, feeling no hunger, no thirst, no pain, no joy, no wonder, no confusion, just a vague feeling of readiness. He touched down in a green grassy field, wandered the field for another hundred years, the field turned to desert and the desert turned to snowy mountainous terrain, and the snowy mountainous terrain made way for more desert and then thick forest and then a sprawling beach. He dove into the water and swam to Paradise Hills, followed the same winding trek he had walked with Mariposita not but two hundred years prior and found himself in front of the very same pyramid he had jumped into two hundred years ago, Mariposita flitting around at the top waiting for him, just as she had promised.

"How'd you like the Biblioteque Paradoxa Infinitu?" Mariposita asked.

"The wha..?"

"Wait when you landed in that grassy field, did you turn left or right?"

"I don't know, right maybe?"

"You were supposed to go left."

He jumped in again, fell another hundred years, landed in the grassy field and turned left.

It was right there, he wondered how he had missed it last time.

Big ass building, maybe a hundred stories high, the architecture had a sort of Tower of Babel vibe.

He wandered into the Biblioteque Paradoxa Infinitu, perused the libros, wandered the aisles of cantos...

The ceilings were high, tall shelves, sliding ladders, spiral staircases, step ladders, the book smell, big windows, plenty of sunlight bouncing verdant-wise off the expansive shrub-enclosed courtyard lawn replete with fountains and hedge mazes, marble, ivy, brick mortar, place, thousands of glittering lamps, and in chambers below, torchlit labyrinthical catacombs, velvet-soaked reading rooms, chambers paradaisical, purgatorial, and otherwise.

Fausto found himself in one of the magazine sections, picked up a copy of Playboy Magazine, read "The Second Bakery Attack" by Haruki Murakami, then he picked up another copy of Playboy Magazine, read "The Handsomest Drowned Man in the World" by Gabriel Garcia Marquez, then he wandered over to one of the literature sections and picked up a copy of Roberto Bolaño's Amulet, read that, then he picked up a copy of Charles Mingus's memoir Beneath the Underdog, read that, then he picked up Jazz by Toni Morrison, reads that, decides he never needs to read another book again, he'll pick up a trumpet and play that.

He played the trumpet for a hundred years, the money poured in, he bought a black '88 Cadillac Fleetwood, threw some of them big rims on it.

He hung his trumpet up, just so he could wander the streets and highways of the Biblioteque Paradoxa Infinitu in his caddy for another hundred years while listening to his hundred-year-long free jazz album.

Right as the hundred-year-long free jazz album ended, the last note skipped and Fausto threw the whip into an infinite donut, its metal and rubber becoming electricity, the electricity becoming nothing, the nothing becoming everything.

For Fausto's next trick, he climbed a mountain, found a cave and decided to live there, subsisting off berries, rainwater and dew. He spent his days walking, taking dips into the icy glacial runoffs, meditating in the sun, napping in the shade.

One morning, while on a walk through a nearby valley,

he stumbled across a mountain lion eating a mountain goat, he scared the mountain lion off by hollering and throwing rocks. He skinned the goat with a sharp rock, built a fire, cooked and ate the goat meat, cleaned the hide, stretched it over the top of a hollow log, made a freegan djembe. He carried the drum back up to his cave and played it for the next hundred years. The acoustics in the cave were beautiful.

As Fausto slapped the djembe for the last time on the closing second of the closing minute of the closing hour of the closing day of the closing week of the closing month of the hundredth year, the drum disintegrated into dust. Fausto coated himself in the dust and meditated for another hundred years, then decided to head over to Paradise Hills to see what Mariposita had been up to the past couple centuries or so.

He stopped into Yoga Azteca, sure enough Mariposita was there, chopping it up with Ife. They received him warmly and they all drink some maté together, then Fausto and Mariposita peace out. They walk around Paradise Hills for 100 years singing the 99 names of Allah and then on the last second of the last minute of the last hour of the last day of the last week of the last month of the last year of the last decade of that century, they kiss, fuck, fall in love, wed, bear 100 children who then each bear 100 more and so on, more branches on that big groovy tree of life, wow. They die a hundred times and a hundred times, they're reborn. Groovy stuff.

3. CADILLAC MOON

Fausto and Mariposita were whipping Fausto's black '88 Cadillac Fleetwood around the moon, peeping the groovy scenery, the trippy moon rock formations, the jet black cosmic roof sprinkled with crazy stars, the earth hanging stupidly in the sky like a big pimple.

They were chill wandering, zig-zagwise, not a goal or intention in sight, pure egoless reception. The radio was playing Thelonious Monk's rendition of "Meet Me Tonight in Dreamland."

"Can the blind see?" Fausto asked Mariposita.

"Yeah," said Mariposita.

"Are all men blind?"

"Yeah."

"What about women?"

"All women have one eye."

"What about butterflies?"

"Butterflies themselves are eyes."

"What is the difference between a woman's eye and the sun?"

"The moon."

"OK, now you ask me a question."

"Do you love me?"

"Yeah."

They drove on for a while, Billie Holiday was singing "Blue Moon" on the radio. She was right, the moon really was blue. So was Fausto's Cadillac now.

Then "Green Onions" by Booker T. and the M.G.'s came on the radio and the Cadillac turned green.

Then "Mellow Yellow" by Donovan came on the radio and the Cadillac turned yellow.

Then "Orange Moon" by Erykah Badu came on the radio and the Cadillac turned orange.

Then "Red Red Wine" by UB40 came on the radio and the Cadillac turned red.

Then "Purple Haze" by Jimi Hendrix came on the radio and Fausto's Cadillac turned purple.

Then "White Light/White Heat" by the Velvet Underground came on the radio and the Cadillac turned white.

Then "Black Heart Man" by Barrington Levy came on and the Cadillac turned back to black.

"An eclectic lil rainbow DJ set," said Mariposita.

"Must be a college station," said Fausto.

"Wonder what it's like to go to college on the moon."

"I got a cousin who went to college on the moon, she said it's fun. The moon's a real party town."

"Let's party then."

They got off at the next exit and hit up a strip club.

"I've never been to a strip club," said Mariposita.

"Moon strip clubs are different, instead of women taking their clothes off and dancing on stage, it's usually just tornadoes of sunflowers."

They went inside and watched the sunflower tornadoes whirl on stage, threw moon dollars, the DJ spun the sound of birds tweeting.

They got a little hotel and and looked up at the dumb ass earth hanging in the sky as they sat in the hot tub on the rooftop pool.

"The moon go hard," said Fausto.

"You ain't never lie," said Mariposita.

The radio was on, playing a song called CADILLAC MOON by THE CADILLAC MOONS.

The sun rose.

4. ORACLE FREESTYLE

Fausto found some work in Oakland as a boxer. He was good at it. Didn't even feel like work. He'd train every day then come home to a meal of flower nectar that Mariposita had collected while he'd been out.

They'd see a movie at Grand Lake, walk the lake, motor around town in the Fleetwood that Fausto was constantly souping up in his spare time. With some minor adjustments to the engine, the lil puppy topped out at around 888 miles per hour. He also added four more wheels and a grand piano.

He was winning every fight by K.O. often in the first round, sometimes with one punch, he had never been knocked down, let alone knocked out. He was like a young Tyson. But boxing was starting to get boring so he decided to do one last fight and call it quits.

His last fight was at the Oracle Arena. His opponent was him. Fausto v. Fausto. It was sold out, everybody in the Bay Area flocked to see Fausto/Fausto. Every bar was playing it, every TV in every household. Fausto versus Fausto, who would win? The odds were 1/1 Fausto, bookies were having a field day.

The first undercard was Kid Jesus v. Elegua competing for the Super Hyphy Weight Belt. Elegua knocked Kid Jesus out with two left jabs and a right hook in the first three seconds of the round, the crowd went dummy.

The second undercard was Disney v. Dali competing for the Heaven Weight Belt. Dali won in an 8th round knockout. It looked like he could've even ended it a few rounds earlier but must have been stretching it out for some backdoor money.

The third undercard was White Jesus v. Olofi competing for the Super Heaven Weight Belt, this one lasted all twelve rounds Olofi whupping the shit out of White Jesus but Jesus refusing to go down. White Jesus landed no punches that whole first eleven rounds, some say he didn't even throw any. In the final seconds of the final round Olofi dropped his gloves and let White Jesus land a right hook on his jaw, and as the paw hit the jaw, Jesus' entire arm combusted into an explosion of blood, like somebody popped a water balloon of Christ's blood. Olofi gave him a left hook and Jesus exploded into a mushroom cloud of blood, soaking the entire audience and leaving just a pair of blood-soaked gloves on the blood-soaked mat as Olof, blood-soaked raised his gloves in victory. The blood-soaked referee licked some blood off of his own finger and announced to the crowd: "It's wine!" The crowd licked themselves drunk. Tough act to follow.

Fabby Davis Junior got up on the mic, announced the title card: Fausto v. Fausto.

"And now, the moment you've all been waiting for, the bout for the Never Wait Championship Belt Fausto Versus Fausto!"

The crowd roared.

"In this corner, in the black trunks, weighing in at 888 fluid hummingbird hearts, with a thousand mile reach and a million mile ice grill, young thunderstruck himself, Fausto!"

The crowded booed.

"And in this corner, in the black trunks, weighing in at 888 fluid hummingbird hearts, with a thousand mile reach and a million mile ice grill, young thunderstruck himself, Fausto!"

The crowded went wild with joy.

"OK gentleman you know the rules, no cussin', no spittin', no animal products, don't take the Lord's name in vain, drink 8 glasses of water a day, honor thy father and thy mother, no timbs, no jays, no sweatpants, no baseball caps, look both ways before you cross the street, brush your teeth at least twice a day, always floss and gargle mouthwash, step on a crack, break ya mama's back, two's company, three's a crowd, three's company too, too much of a good thing is a bad thing, always wash ur hands, keep ya head up, no foul facial gestures, overstand the science immaculate, energy equals mass times the speed of light squared, scared money don't make no money, leaves of three let it be, if u gota take a chance get the dough in advance, it is what it was and will be, only real player pimpologies, cold heart, iceberg hot heat flames, the game is to be sold not told, increase the peace, Peace in the Middle East, Peace is the Answer, Praise Buddha, Allah Jesus Etc., fuck with the vision fam, yadda yadda yadda, now touch gloves and let's have us a clean fight boys, really go at it and show those fuckers out there what that raw blood and guts shit really look like."

Fausto and Fausto stood locked in a steely-eyed star-edown through the quick intro then bumped gloves and hit they lil corners, bell rang, they came out, sat down at a wooden table. On the table was a glass jar holding two fresh cut sunflowers sitting in vapor-distilled holy water and two plates, each holding a single triangular watermelon slice.

Fausto and Fausto removed their gloves and ate the watermelon.

Fausto won, Fausto lost.

FAUSTO BOMAYE!

"And the winner by way of metaphysical knockout is… Fausto!"

The crowd went wild with joy, rage, confusion, they turned to a brite wite lite and then into a deep black dark.

5. YIPIN

Fausto was yipin out the cutterinos yipped offa nit nit bree bree tizznoe bray bray africo italo allah yahweh yummin on yuckers and what nizznot, he was out there somewhere in the ruffianical corners, scraping the diamonds off the top of the cave ceiling, furl meh, they was twisted up littydocious furl and smurl, dummied out film flammin and lambastin go axe about it, the mannish manes went heckof maney, super duper hyphadocious crackalackin nizznucks and whizznippin cadillacs through southernplaylistical lanscapes, scrapin thru north cackalacka peace allah jacka, diagonal sliding through avenues, snackin and smacking, jackin and mackin, mobbin, smobbin, shmobbin even, stylish, styley, style-esque, the shred continued in such a manner so as to bestow a sense of willingness to proceed yet even further thusly the shred did indeed, alas, continue, he slooped goofylike, tree wizened, lackadaisical, soaking the ever-present gamifications rambling and perambulating ziggin, zaggin, jiggin, jaggin, giggin, guffawin, pawin dangling bells of existence, exploding skeletal from the skin sheathes, finessin the bowl, gleaming the cube, reelin in the yurrz, pouring hot dead ancient ashes of the ancestral barkers long past and gone from the urn of the mental domepiece, true gasping linguistic knowledges, the flapping of wings within cages, the bird songz, chirpin, yurpin, tweetin, skeetin, creepin, gleeshin, geekin, freakin, fleekin, skreekin, hawky, shocky, the fortuitous, fortunado, oportunidades, the blistering beaks of the birds of reality, the whip cracks, the seedlings, splashes of dirt and blood, cold stone actualities, choking spermologies, quotidian breads, pans, pains, perks and jerks, corky rumination of wood and wine, leaf green laffers and loafers alike, the push and pull the wiggling, wriggling free sunlite, sun kisses, moon kisses, spearmint forests, replete with wild flamboyant birds, toucanical tusks, flappin bat beasts, snarlin tapirs, the chunky spirit of the love, the spite, the spit, the spasms, paroxysms, the waving of limbs, gazebos, underworlds, underwears, spitting sprites and spirits rolling out their lavish whip tongues, gargantuan butterfly philosophies, the howling red hot winds of the hellish heavens of the desert island earth, the sun diamonds mined from the soul's interior magnetic magmic magic magnanimous cavernous regions, the moon rox, plopped like tears from eyeballs, the great fibers, the skrangs, stringy and singy, the sparkling sparks, nagchamipcal logix, the codexes of intrepid futures and pasts, like wow.

6. OH MY FUCKIN GOD

Fausto and Mariposita were walking through the Mental Avian Museum of Art in New Golgotha, talking art.

"What is art?"

"What isn't?"

"What's your favorite art?"

"Life, what's yours?"

"Death."

"What's the difference between life and death?"

"Truth."

"What's the difference between truth?"

"Itself."

"What is?"

"What isn't?"

"What isn't?"

"What is?"

"Is is is?"

"Is is."

"Is is?"

"Yes."

"Yes or no?"

"Yes."

"Why?"

"Why not."

"What isn't?"

"Isn't."

"Is isn't is?"

"Yes."

"Is yes?"

"Yes, yes is."

"What else?"

"Nothing."

"And?"

"And…"

"Everything?"

"Yes."

"Yes is everything?"

"Everything is yes."

"What is what?"

"What?"

"What is everything?"

"What is anything?"

"If is is is and isn't is is, is is isn't?"

"Yes, is is isn't."

"Everything isn't?"

"Everything isn't."

"Everything is?"

"Everything is."

"Everything?"

"Everything."

"Everything?"

"Everything?"

"Everything."

"What about about?"

"What about about?"

"What about it?"

"What, about?"

"No, it."

"It is."

"What about is?"

"What is is about?"

"Is is about is"

"About is about about."

"Everything is about everything."

"Everything is everything."

"Everything is."

"Everything."

"Is."

"How about how?"

"How about what?"

"How?"

"What about how?"

"How about how?"

"Why?"

"Because… how?"

"How?"

"Yes."

"What is how about?"

"What isn't?"

"What?"

"Because…"

"Why because?"

"How is why?"

"Why is how?"

"Why is how?"

"No."

"Huh…"

"Ha."

"Hahahaha."

"Hahahahaha."

"Hahahahahahahaha!"

"Hahahahahahahahahahahaha!"

"HAHAHAHAHAHAHAHAHAHAHAHAHA!"

"HAHAHAHAHAHAHAHAHAHAHAHAHAHAHA-HAHA!"

7. CHICORY

Fausto and Mariposita stood in a field of chicory contemplating the hazy noncommittal nature of the purplish blue (or bluish purple), seeming to shift from one to the other in front of one's very eyes due to slight changes in light, wind, sense of self, swell and ebb of time, angle, context, hydration, it was a trip, the shimmering ethereal between states, the liminal half hues, something else entirely, everything else even. They recalled their metaphilosophical convo at the art gallery and calmly breathed in and out gazing upon the chicory. What a naughty lil daisy, whimsical with a rebel yell, a sweet lil funky lil flower, baby wowee.

"This flower is the realest art," they said in unison.

"This flower is the purest beauty," they said in unison.

"This flower is the highest power," they said in unison.

"This flower is the truest knowledge," they said in unison.

"This flower contains multitudes," they said in unison.

"This flower is love's most powerful weapon," they said in unison.

"This flower is an agent of peace," they said in unison.

"This flower is a vivid yin yang," they said in unison.

"This flower is a potent magic," they said in unison.

"This flower is the most perfect philosophy," they said in unison.

"This flower has broken the world's heart," they said in unison.

"This flower, even in death, will never diminish in value," they said in unison.

"This flower is beyond the reach of human rationale," they said in unison.

"This flower is governed by no law of man," they said in unison.

"This flower is compassionate," they said in unison.

"This flower behaves as if it has nothing to lose," they said in unison.

8. WHAT U THOUGHT THO

Fausto was over at Chuck Freight's house in True Valley, drinking palm wine and politicking.

"This palm wine go hard, Chuck, where you get it?"

"My new job at the Haunted Palm Orchard."

"Oh word you quit the post office?"

"Yeah, finally."

"So the wine is haunted?"

"Naw just the orchard."

"Huh…"

"I mean maybe the wine too, I don't know, I imagine little ghosts might fall into the vats sometimes."

"Yeah, I'd figure as much."

"Yeah…"

"Kinda tastes haunted…"

"You think?"

"Yeah…"

Chuck took another sip.

"Naw, I don't taste any ghosts…"

"Tasted kinda haunted to me."

"Agree to disagree…"

They sat drinking, lil Fausto had an idea.

"Ay, I got an idea."

"What?"

"We should have a drinking contest."

"Huh?"

"Like a contest to see who can drink more."

"I thought that's what we were doing."

"Naw, it wasn't official, we didn't shake hands on no rules or nothing."

"OK, so what's the rules?"

"Whoever drinks more wins."

"Bet."

They shook on it and continued to drink.

They drank til the sun came up and they drank all day and on into the night and the next day, and the day after that, just drinking all of the free haunted palm wine Chuck had swiped from his job at the Haunted Palm Orchard and listening to whatever was on the radio, rapping about whatever.

On the hundredth day, Fausto won: Chuck Freight took his last sip of palm wine and died. His spirit jumped out of his body and flew off to the Land of the Dead.

Fausto sat, drunk as a skunk, blinking in shock for a second. Through the haze of the palm wine, he remembered a story his pops told him once about how pretty much the same thing had happened to him. Pops had been drinking palm wine with his palm wine tapster homie and dude just up and died, spirit flew off to the Land of the Dead.

Apparently, young Fausto had learned nothing from this cautionary tale.

But wait, there was more…

His pops also said he had journeyed to the Land of the Dead and brought dude back. So all Fausto had to do was travel to the Land of the Dead…

9. SKULLDUGGERY

Fausto was zipping through the Land of the Dead on a 197777777 Harley Daemonson Road Wizard motorcycle.

The Land of the Dead was actually quite beautiful, a lot of gray desert with white skies and jungles of black trees, cities scattered here and there, an endless gray maze, filled with devils, dead people, spirits, ghosts, skeletons and the like. But very beautiful.

Fausto pulled over at a gas station to fill up.

"How far is Dead Town? I ain't seen no signs in hella long," he asked a Desert Spirit gassing his pickup.

The Desert Spirit just shrugged and gazed off into the distance.

Fausto bought a pack of bubblegum and roared off.

He rolled into Dead Town at night, ready to kick ass and chew bubblegum and he was all out of bubblegum. Dead Town was all lit up, neon lights, the screams of ghosts, et cetera, et cetera.

Fausto walked into a saloon and ordered a shot of bourbon, threw that back and watched a skeleton piano player tinkle the ivories, soulful, monkish, dutiful carvings of ordered sound onto the air.

Fausto hit up Dead Town Casino, got drunk and got to shooting dice, one thing led to another and before he knew it, a Dice Spirit had pulled a knife on him.

All of a sudden, five devils ran up, one holding a wooden table, another two holding wooden chairs, another holding a glass jar with two fresh cut sunflowers, and the last holding two white ceramic plates, each containing a single, triangular slice of watermelon.

Fausto and the Dice Spirit sat down and supped on the watermelon. A crowd gathered.

"Looks like we have ourselves a good old fashioned watermelon eating contest!" some devil shouted, and immediately devils and deads alike lined up to bet.

Fausto and the Dice Spirit ate watermelon for a hundred days and in the final second of the final minute of the final hour of the hundredth day, the Dice Spirit took his last bite of watermelon and keeled over dead.

A jungle spirit who made 500k betting on Fausto was so happy he won that he granted Fausto one wish.

Fausto said: "I wish to bring my dead homie Chuck back from the Land of the Dead."

And like that, Fausto and Chuck were back at Chuck's house in True Valley.

"Think you were right, Fausto, that wine was haunted,"

Chuck said as he cracked some palm wine, "Now how bout another drinkin' contest?"

10. CLASSIC

Fausto and Mariposita were in the Cornelius Cornwall Thornbottom Hall for Fine Classical and Operatic Musics, listening to a lil chamber orchestra perform Ludwig Rainier Maria Von Trilke's Trillepathy for Several Seasons, the Devil's Repose in the Angel's Desert Campground; Sonata in Q Diagonal Majorus-Metti-Minorus, Third through Three Hundred-and-Thirty-Third movements, Adante Allegroza, Bellisima.

The conductor, Maestro Don Ricardo Rigatonni-Rodriguez-Madera-Von-Trilke De La Vazquez-Velazquez-Solsona-Rosales-Chinaski-Ben-Salad-Al-Assad-Wong (B.K.A. Lil Ricky) was a distant relative of the composer through a complicated multinational lineage too tedious to recount here. Needless to say he was a real rockstar, an infamous character in the parlors of the elite, eliciting mixed, but always relatively animated, reactions when brought up in conversation.

The players were as follows:

Piano: Esmerelda Perron-LochViolin (First Chair): Pema FofangViolin (Second Chair): Dill PurtainsViolin (Third Chair): Deseret Yukio Viola (First Chair): Pantera ZhouViola (Second Chair): Roy Rogers (no relation)Cello: Marcello LimoncelloDouble Bass: Winton Seraphim-Flute (First Chair): Sammy Sosa (no relation)Flute (Second Chair): Chinga TumadreFlute (Third Chair): Ladybird Los AngelesPan Pipes: Sun KimVibraphone: Mark LingThe Pain: Error TerrorThe Joys (First Chair): Cheepie McBride-The Joys (Second Chair): Yogi ZeroClarinet (First Chair):

Sally Jessie DonatelloClarinet (Second Chair): Courtney KotaOboe:Corky Valdez-PinotTrumpet (First Chair): Jinx AnimeTrumpet (Second Chair)· Donald QuarteiTuba: Bill BintParadox (First Chair): Reginald SinghParadox (Second Chair): Yun-Yi LiuTimpani: Velma PantooeyCymbals: Church John ChunkWatermelon Slice (First Chair): Fausto FaustoWatermelon Slice (Second Chair): Fausto Fausto

The symphony lasted 44 hours of pure mind boggling sublime metanoia and in the final seconds of the final minute of the final hour, Fausto Fausto & Fausto Fausto, seated across each other at a wooden table set with a glass of vapor distilled holy water holding two sunflowers, lifted their triangular watermelon slices in unison and ate them.

Fausto watched rapt from the audience, tears rolling down his face. Mariposita, who had fallen asleep on his shoulder, woke up and politely clapped.

11. THIRTY THREE

Fausto and Mariposita went on a date to the Basonic Lodge Cafe in Brett Cooke-Dizneyland in Tianeman Gardens, Mollywood.

Fausto ordered an apple and a glass of water, Mariposita ordered a flower, whatever they had, the house flower.

They ate in silence and then sat in deep meditation for the next 33 hours, 33 minutes and 33 seconds.

On the 33rd second of the 33rd minute of the 33rd hour, they opened their eyes and their surroundings had vanished, their table was floating above a calm blue ocean, set with two triangular watermelon slices. They ate their watermelon slices and exploded in twin mushroom clouds of blood, staining the deep blue ocean a vibrant purple.

The purple waves seethed and surged, spat foam, hissed,

leapt into the air, churned, gathered into massive rolling hills, towering walls, crashing into white frothy breaks, a billowing, violent pleasance, the liquid sheets of matter, shimmering with existential conviction, whispering exact blueprints of the perfect cosmic god energy with every silken pose and utterance, every undulating thrust of its fluid, ever-changing person, prismatically polyphysically transmogrifying its multitudinous pan morphologies and magnanimous ambulations into the infinitely sphere of totality, etc. etc.

They ended up in Hotel Cinco Sensos in Los Santos, Republica Democratica de Los Isles Motocicletas, having sex.

When a butterfly has sex with a man, the butterfly lands on the man's erect penis and sits motionless for 33 hours, 33 minutes, and 33 seconds, until both parties explode into twin mushroom clouds of blood, destroying and rebirthing the universe and living the entirety of its existence back to that very same moment. It's pretty intense and not for the uninitiated.

So anyway, they did that.

And they gave birth right there to an island, named the island Perlita, and lived there for a while, swimming, eating mangoes, drinking coconut water.

And then they swam off somewhere else.

12. TWENTY-THREE

Fausto was wandering around a video game arcade, contact blitted off the various vapors and ethers, he hooked himself up to a virtual reality game called Be Anybody You Want To Be.

He chose to be Michael Jordan.

He dunked on hella fools.
Then he was Kareem Abdul-Jabbar.
Dunked on hella fools.
Then he was Wilt Chamberlain.
Dunked on hella fools.
Then he was Magic Johnson.
Dunked on hella fools.
Then he was Shaquille O'Neal
Dunked on hella fools.

And so on and so forth; Allen Iverson, Carmelo Anthony, Charles Barkley, Bill Russell, Mitch Richmond, Antawn Jamison, Chris Mullin, Tim Hardaway, Steph Curry, Kevin Durant, Draymond Green, Russell Westbrook, Lebron James, Kobe Bryant, Scottie Pippen, Horace Grant, Kawhi Leonard, Isaiah Thomas, James Harden, Hakeem Olajuwon, Muhammad Ali, Mike Tyson, Sugar Ray Leonard, Jack Johnson, Jackie Robinson, Willie Mays, Barry Bonds, Jose Canseco, Pele, Cristiano Ronaldo, Lionel Messi, Pope John Paul II, Pope Francis, Marcus Garvey, Elijah Muhammad, Karl Marx, Lao Tzu, Che Guevara, Malcolm X, Martin Luther King, Jesus Christ, Mohammad, Jimi Hendrix, Bob Marley, James Brown, John Coltrane, Miles Davis, Thelonious Monk, Bud Powell, Cannonball Adderley, Sun Ra, Ornette Coleman, Cecil Taylor, Stevie Wonder, Ray Charles, Roberto Bolano, Haruki Murakami, Jean Michel-Basquiat, Hermann Hesse, Chinua Achebe, Keith Haring, Marvin Gaye, Al Green, Otis Redding, Chuck Berry, Little Richard, Bobby Blue Bland, Lightnin Hopkins, Muddy Waters, B.B. King, Johnny Hartman, Prince, Sly Stone, 2Pac, E-40, Mac Dre, Too Short, Ice Cube, Rappin 4-Tay, Shock G, Del Tha Funkee Homosapien, Keak Da Sneak, San Quinn, C-Bo, Ant Banks, Rammellzee, MF Doom, Lil Wayne, Juvenile, BG, Turk, Bulletproof, Birdman, Mannie Fresh, Master P, Silkk the Shocker, C Murder, Mystikal, Kool Keith, Lil B, Yung L, Stunnaman, Lil Uno, Casual, Phesto, Opio, A-Plus,

Tajai, Andre Nickatina, Mistah Fab, Equipto, Nef The Pharaoh, MURS, The Grouch, Sunspot Jonz, Eligh, Bicasso, Aesop, Scarub, Luckyjam, Scarface, Pimp C, Bun B, Project Pat, Juicy J, Killer Mike, Andre 3000, Big Boi, Devin Tha Dude, Z-Ro, Slim Thug, Rakim, Kool G Rap, Biggie, KRS-ONE, Big Pun, Chuck D, B Real, Snoop Dogg, Slick Rick, Q-Tip, Phife, Prodigy, Havoc, Nas, Jay-Z, Jaz-O, Dame Dash, Cam'ron, Juelz Santana, Jim Jones, Hell Rell, Freaky Zeek, Carlos Santana, Ghostface Killah, Raekwon, Method Man, Ol' Dirty Bastard, GZA, RZA, Cappadonna, Inspectah Deck, Redman, U-God, Masta Killa, Killa Priest, Jada Kiss, Styles P, Sheek Louch, Mos Def, Talib Kweli, Kanye West, Black Thought, Questlove, Danny Brown, Mr. Muthafuckin Exquire, A$AP Rocky, A$AP Yams, Tray 357, Ease Da Man, Polo, Puzzle, Bizzy Bone, Krayzie Bone, Layzie Bone, Wish Bone, Flesh-N-Bone, Wiz Khalifa, Royce Da 5'9, Guilty Simpson, A.G. The Coroner, Dopehead, Chavis Chandler, Sheefy McFly, Illingsworth, Soulja Boy, Quavo, Takeoff, Offset, Schoolly D, Camu Tao, Fat Lip, Imani, Bootie Brown, Slimkid3, Biz Markie, Prince Paul, Ad Rock, MCA, Mike D, KOOL A.D., Kurt Cobain, Little Bruce, Loren Hell, Amaze 88, Squadda B, Mondre Man, Trackademicks, 1-O.A.K., Iamsu, Dave Steezy, Cousin Fik, Lil Zee, Ezale, El P, Big Juss, Mr. Len, Despot, Gunplay, Fat Trel, Fredo Santana, Common, Twista, Fat Tony, Droop-E, Issue, Mysonne, Emmanuel Jal, Immortal Technique, Zach De La Roca, Epic, Illekt, Jasson, Uncle Murdah, Red Cafe, Maino, Jabee, Lantana, Beanie Sigel, Memph Bleek, Freeway, Murda Mook, Cassidy, Stalley, Meyhem Lauren, Homeboy Sandman, Blu, Oddisee, Joey Badass, Jah Jah, Telli, MC Ride, Action Bronson, Tyga, Theophilus London, Kid Cudi, Dr. Dre, Eminem, Chief Keef, Prince Be, Fresh Prince, Cheech Marin, Tommy Chong, Chamillionaire, Mix Master Mike, Junior Vazquez, James Baldwin, Kurt Russell, Kevin Costner, Jules Feiffer, Val Kilmer,

Ricky Powell, Money Mark, John C. Reilly, Play, Kid, Sway, Tech, Dapwell, Lakutis, Mike Finito, DJ Red Alert, Funk Flex, Mr. Cee, Big Baby Gandhi, Le'roy Benros, Busdriver, Verbs, Creature, Open Mike Eagle, Chaz Van Queen, Kassa Overall, Keyboard Kid, Nacho Picasso, Maffew Ragazino, Quelle Christopher, Raheem Recess, Niko Is, CX Kidtronik, Beans, High Priest, M. Sayyid, Earl Blaize, Lil Yachty, Playboi Carti, Desiigner, DVS, Plinio, Eskay, Final Outlaw, Poison Pen, Dallas Penn, Ted Bono, Combat Jack, Tone Tank, Harry Fraud, Steel Tipped Dove, Isaiah Toothtaker, Baje One, Ceschi, Nabahe, Aesop Rock, Sole, Jel, Lynas, Scott Thorough, Disaster, Aaron Cohen, Iron Solomon, Ricky Powell, Edan, Clams Casino, French Montana, Max B, Lil B again, Joe Budden, KOOL A.D. again, Jim Morrison, every member of Creedence Clearwater Revival, one at a time, every member of Creedence Clearwater Revival at the same time, then that same thing again but with Tower of Power this time, David Bowie, Mick Jagger, Keith RIchards, Brian Jones, John Lennon, Paul McCartney, George Harrison, Ringo Starr, Stuart Sutcliffe, Pete Shotton, Derek Taylor, Neil Aspinall, George Martin, Brian Epstein, Brian Wilson, Phil Spector, Richard Hell, David Byrne, Arthur Russell, Brian Eno, Kilo Ali, Cameo, Barry Gordy, LMFAO, 50 Cent, Ja Rule, LL Cool J, Canibus, Kool Moe Dee, DJ Kool Herc, Kool Keith again, KOOL A.D. again, Meek Mill, Drake, Eli Porter, Wesley Willis, Fyodor Dostoevsky, Ernest Hemingway, Ralph Ellison, Richard Wright, David Foster Wallace, Yukio Mishima, Bugs Bunny, Michael Jordan again, Muhammad Ali again, etc.

Then he decided to be himself.

Fausto Fausto.

And he realized that's what the whole game was about.

He was himself.

Fausto Fausto.

Himself.

He had won.

He was himself.

He had won the game.

He had won Be Anybody You Want To Be.

He unhooked himself from the Virtual Reality harness-es. Or did he? There was no way to tell, the fabricated reality was too exact. Regardless, from that point on, it didn't make a difference if he had or if he hadn't. He had won the game, he was himself.

He was, and would forever be: Fausto Fausto.

13. KICKED OFF

Fausto and Mariposita were posted up in a loft in Nuevo Texarkana, Nueva Mixtlan, watching the homie Chuck Freight on TV, he had made it onto hit reality show The Island of Death, a show where 100 contestants compete to be the last living person on a booby-trapped island teem-ing with deadly animals and armed drones. To liven things up, all contestants are abducted without warning from their sleep and thrust into this landscape of unimaginable terrors with no explanation of what was going on.

This was the season finale and Chuck was doing well on the show given the circumstances, he was among the last thirteen people alive. Apparently twelve people had to die this episode. We hoped none of them were Chuck. Chuck's track record was actually pretty remarkable so far, he hadn't killed any people or even animals — he had maimed a tiger in self defense, an understandable transgression — and he had shot down a bunch of drones with a rifle he had taken from some dead dude and was hiding out in what looked to be a pretty safe and comfortable cave, basically waiting for everybody else to kill each other. Very relatable television.

Mariposita found it too stressful. "Turn it off," she said, "I can't take watching it."

"Neither can I, but I can't turn it off, that's the homie," said Fausto.

So they sat there watching the terror.

"This is the worst show on television," said Mariposita.

"I think he's gonna make it," said Fausto.

No sooner than he'd said that, a drone flew into Chuck's cave and shot him in the head.

"Damn, poor Chuck can't catch a break," said Fausto. He bid adieu to Mariposita and hopped on his Harley, set out for the Land of the Dead.

14. AUDIO VIDEO DISCO

Back in the Land of the Dead, Fausto decided, on a hunch, to hit Upper Deadsville, a bar called One Punch, being that Chuck used to date one of the bartenders there, Candi.

He walked in and, of course, guess who he sees at the bar:

"Chuck! Boy am I glad to see you!"

"You saw the show huh?"

"Crazy stuff man, that hurt?"

"Naw, all happened too fast."

"Horrible show."

"Terrible."

"I can't see it lasting longer than a few more seasons."

"Who knows, the world sucks."

"True."

Candi walks up, "What are you boys having?"

"Candi! Fancy meeting you here"

"Chuck! If I knew it was you I'da broke a bottle over your good-for-nothing ass head!"

"At least it'd be some attention."

"Sup Candi."

"Hey Fausto, whatchall having?"

"Beers."

She left came back with some Dead Flowers Ale. "They're on his tab," she said to Fausto and turned to Chuck winking, "We'll settle that later."

They knocked back the cold ones presented to them, got two more.

"How's the butterfly?"

"She's good."

"No doubt."

Then guess who came in the door?

"Yogi Zero!"

"Bless!"

"Can we get you a beer?"

"Naw, I'm getting an Aztec Yoga."

"Wuzzat."

"Fresh watermelon juice and tequila añejo."

"Sounds nice, let's get a round of those."

They did, caught up.

"This drink do its thing."

"It also works with mescal or ron oscuro."

"Good looks."

"What you up to now, Zero."

"Aztec Yoga."

"Oh word yeah, I'm up on that too," said Fausto.

"Me too," said Chuck.

"Naw, not the drink, Chuck," said Fausto.

"I'll have to show y'all some moves some time," said Yogi Zero.

"No doubt."

"No doubt."

"Saw you on Island of Death man."

"Don't remind me."

The night wore on, they continued to drink.

Yogi Zero ended up showing some Aztec Yoga moves right then and there at the bar to Fausto and Chuck. Candi got involved too. They ran through a few: The Thoughtful Bat, Huitzilopotchtli's Harpoon, Tezacalipoca Prana, The Thirsty Fish, The Evil Cobra, The Laughing Cobra, Coatlicue's Necklace, Kung Fu Yoga, The Forever Ring, The Fire Flame Hardbody Karate, The Peyote Karaoke, The O.G. Aztec Yoga Move #1, The Finesse, The Zig Zag Zig, The Spanish Castle Magic, etc., they were invigorating and wild spiritually instructive.

"Come visit my temple out in Los Discos."

"No doubt."

"Ay let's hit Peyote Karaoke," said Chuck, "Candi, what time you get off?"

"Right now."

They headed over to Peyote Karaoke (the karaoke bar, not the Aztec Yoga move, but, in many ways, also the Aztec Yoga move), which was over in Murder Town, which wasn't as bad as the name made it sound, but a lot of places in the Land of the Dead were like that. Fausto hollered at Mariposita and told her to slide through too, she met them over there.

They got a lil video booth.

Yogi Zero went first and did "Everybody Wants to Rule the World" by Tears for Fears.

Then Candi did "Material Girl" by Madonna.

Then Chuck Freight did "Don't Stop Believin'" by Journey.

Then Fausto did "When You Were Mine" by Prince.

Then Mariposita did Trillepathy for Several Seasons, the Devil's Repose in the Angel's Desert Campground; Sonata in Q Diagonal Majorus-Metti-Minorus, Third through Three Hundred-and-Thirty-Third movements, Adante Allegroza, Bellisima.

They all turned into triangular slices of watermelon and ate themselves, exploded into five mushroom clouds of blood and disintegrated into a bride wite lite and faded into a deep dark black.

15. GHETTO ARCHITECTURE

Fausto was spending a night in the clink. He'd had too much to drink at Peyote Karaoke last night and on the way back from taking a piss he'd gotten into some kind of scuffle that led to him getting escorted out of the premises in handcuffs, blood on him, some his, some foreign. He didn't remember the details. He didn't know what time it was.

A one-eyed ghost came up and sat down next to him on the bench that he (even while black out drunk) had had the presence of mind to snatch up early on.

"Name's Evil Eye Pete."

"Which one?"

"Excuse me?"

"Which eye is evil, the one you got or the one that got away?"

"Evil is relative."

"What you in for?"

"Card sharking, you?"

"Fighting, I think, I don't remember."

"Doesn't matter anyway."

"What does?"

"Nothin."

"Amen, brother."

They sat in silence.

Two little goblins fought each other, a couple skeletons broke it up.

Somebody farted.

The apprehended wrongdoers sat mumbling, coughing, farting, trying to fall asleep sitting, fall asleep standing, fall asleep on the floor, wherever they could

They were led to another cell, saw public defenders, and were led two by two into the courtroom.

The judge was the Venerable Judge Screaming Sampson (a giant devil, 666 feet tall, who spoke only in a blood-curdling scream), who was handing out life in jail like it was candy.

When it was Fausto's turn before the Honorable Judge Screaming Sampson, he cleared his throat and began a monologue he had prepared for exactly such an occasion:

"Ahem… Your Honor, if it would please the court—"

"SILENCE! INSUBORDINATION! 666 YEARS!"

He was thrown in solitary, no light, no bed, bread and water once a day. He lived in deep meditation for 666 years and on the final second of the final minute of the final hour of the final day of the final week of the final month of the final year, the guard brought him a single, triangular slice of watermelon. Fausto ate it and exploded into a mushroom cloud of blood that disintegrated into a brite wite lite which faded into a deep dark black.

16. THUGGADELLIC DREAMS

Fausto and Mariposita were rolling through the town in a jade green 197777777 Caddy Seville.

The sky was a beautiful jade caddy green, the sun a blazing verdant emerald green, the clouds, a bulbous billowing cotton candy apple green, verde, smurl meh, duro verde.

The green sheen shaned pon errythang. Verdant, bellixima. Trooey Gooey, the melty language of lite.

The town was on, brilliating, solar, lit, green as green

get. The styles of the town was wild floral, leafy, viney, crawling with vines, ready to explode with florality.

They hit a liquor store, got a few lotto scratchers, a pack of Kools and a big Jack Daniels, they were shooting for a real vibe here.

They went to a motel, watched TV, scratched lotto tickets, drank whiskey, smoked cigarettes, had butterfly sex. They won a couple hundred bucks off the lotto tickets.

Went back to the liquor store, bought all their porno mags, plus scissors and glue; then they hit up a little bookstore, Ben's Books, and bought a copy of War & Peace, went back to the motel and made little porno collages on every page of War & Peace.

Then they flipped through their book, feeling like aroused artistic geniuses.

They made butterfly love again and watched some more TV.

On TV was a strange little TV show. The show was called Fausto and Mariposita Watching TV and it was just Fausto and and Mariposita sitting right there in that very same motel room, watching TV.

It started to get boring and they were about to change the channel when on the show, Fausto and Mariposita got up, put some clothes on and went outside. They hopped into a red '19666666 Cadillac DeVille and rolled around town, brilliating like the ruby sun hanging in the crimson sky.

They drove off a cliff into a boiling red ocean and sunk to the bottom, hit an underwater liquor store, copped some Patron Añejo, went to an underwater motel, got drunk, had butterfly sex, watched TV.

On TV was, trippy enuff, a show called Fausto and Mariposita Watching TV Underwater and which consisted of, predictably, just Fausto and Mariposita watching TV in that very same underwater motel room.

They watched for a while and just as Fausto was about to change the channel, TV Fausto and TV Mariposita got up and went outside, hopped in their blue '99 Cadillac DeVille and whipped around under the deep blue ocean, brilliating like azure water suns, hit the liquor stoe, pict up sum Henny and hit a mo'tel, had butterfly sex, watched TV.

This time the TV show was them in a yurple room, eating triangular yurple watermelon slices.

"TV zux," said Mariposita.

They turned off the TV, smasht, and fell asleep.

Weird date.

17. GO BANANAS

Yogi Zero invited Fausto, Mariposita, Chuck, and Candi to The Yogi Zero Temple of the Yoga Azteca and Subsidiary Arts, Sciences & Philosophies out in Los Discos, to participate in a group meditation and Aztec Yoga sesh.

They arrived at the temple and were escorted to the backyard by a lady named Parahamsa Wind. She had a third eye, blinking right there in the middle of her forehead.

The backyard had a spacious lawn enclosed within the protective huddle of sixteen willow trees, a few acres of fruit trees (bananas, apples, oranges, lemons, peaches, nectarines, plums, pears, etc.) zigzagging in labyrinths beyond the willows, and just past those, some casitas where various staffers and devotees lived. About two dozen people were sitting cross-legged on the lawn in a big circle, Yogi Zero proclamating a bit, as he was prone to do before a sesh, essentially filibustering as the lawn filled up with more devotees:

"...La Magia, La Magia, La Magia, language is metaphor, meta four is five, five is man, power, refinement, the animal presupposes its own ghost, five fingers on the hand there is no need for words, no need for sound, no need for language, no need for intellect, no need for feeling, no need for need, no need for no, no need for anything, no need for me, no need for you, you're me, I'm you, we're us, there's no us, we're not here, here is not here, there is not there, here is there is nowhere is everything, everything is everything is nothing is anything is you is me is us, OK, looks like that's everybody, let's start out with some meditation."

Everybody sat in silent meditation for an hour and then the Aztec Yoga started:

"OK, now everybody lift one leg off of the ground, now the other, now lift your third leg. Touch your third eye with your third thumb, look into the sun's third soul and breathe."

They did as they were told.

They did the Quetzalcoatl Uttanasana, the Chalchiuht-licue Navasana, the Tialoc Twist, the Cartesian Tabernacle, the Huitzilopotchtli Cha Cha, the Zig Zag Zig Allah, the Trippy Jumping Jack, the Slingblade, the Prana Dada, the Landing Gear, the Oochie Wallie, the Corner Store Bop, the Metzli Marjaryasana, etc., etc.

They expanded every hidden invisible metaphysical organ in their existential pantheon. A major group slay. Everybody vibin, killin it, doin' the thang, Aztec Yoga baby.

18. ENJOY THE MAGNAMITY

Post-sesh, after the last of the devout Yogi Zero followers traipsed off to their casitas or else jumped in their whips back home elsewhere, Fausto, Mariposita, Chuck, and Candi remained, shooting the shucks with Zero.

"Man, Zero, I had no idea you had it like this," said Chuck.

"Yeah man," said Fausto.

"I cleansed my soul, spirit and aura y'all, I wandered mother earth spring-fresh, a new born babe, allowing her to bless me with her fruitful bounty."

"That's a funny way of saying your rich grandpa finally died."

"Har-dee-har-har, joker. Death is nothing, nothing is everything, everything is everything, my grandpa is your grandpa and our grandpa is us, we are infinite, incapable of death..."

Candi whispered to Chuck, "Wait, did his grandpa really die?"

"I don't know, I was making an educated guess," he whispered back.

Yogi Zero gave his guests a tour of the orchards, pontificating and yammering on about this or that mystical hoo-ha:

"..Life is a fog, a mist, a fluctuating cloud of nonsense, here at The Yogi Zero Temple of the Yoga Azteca we aim to tap dance on the clouds of existence with shoes made of pure light. The light is generated from your soul's sun."

"Interesting..." said Mariposita.

"Over here is a peach tree, try one of them puppies on for size."

They all ate peaches, the peaches were insane, brilliant, very good peaches.

"You run a tight ship over here, Zero."

"Ya tu sabe my brutha."

They entered the temple proper and Yogi Zero pointed out the various statuettes and idols and their spiritual significances.

"Who's the Pope in this sprawling theology?" asked Chucko.

"There's no Pope in Yoga Azteca, no big homie in the sky either, just a bunch of lil homies, gods, saints, demigods, bodhisattvas, priests, priestesses, monks, nuns, baba-laos, witch doctors, shamans, et. al... Anyway, moving on, here we have Santo Drasnius Dubiaku Xolotl, a spry jumper who leapt over the chasm of death into a plane of eternal joy and happiness, he's a trickster and good luck when traveling by boat, aeroplane or flying saucer... and over here is Santa Xochiquetzal Rati de Alexandria, the goddess of calm sex and weird surprises, her totem is a man's bowler hat..."

And so on and so forth. An illuminating monologue if at times a touch didactic.

They retired to some guest casitas behind the orchards for the night.

"Enjoy the magnamity," said Yoga Zero as he headed off to his own cabin.

19. GOD FISH

They awoke to the chiming of bells, wandered back to the lawn where the meditation was held the previous night, and had a breakfast of fresh picked fruit salad and green tea on a long table that had been set up by some of the burlier devotees.

Parahamsa Wind was at the rhetorical lectern today, she was all like:

"भाषा रूपक है, मेटा चार पांच है, पांच मनुष्य है, शक्ति, परिशोधन, पशु अपना भूत मानता है, शब्दों की कोई ज़रूरत नहीं, ध्वनि की कोई आवश्यकता नहीं, भाषा की कोई ज़रूरत नहीं, बुद्धि की आवश्यकता नहीं, महसूस करने की कोई आवश्यकता नहीं है, ज़रूरत के लिए कोई ज़रूरत नहीं, कोई ज़रूरत नहीं, कोई ज़रूरत नहीं, मेरे लिए कोई ज़रूरत नहीं, तुम्हारे लिए कोई ज़रूरत नहीं है, आप मुझे हैं, मैं हूं, हम हम हैं, कोई नहीं, हम यहाँ नहीं हैं, यहाँ नहीं है, वहां नहीं है,

यहां है, कहीं नहीं है सब कुछ है, सब कुछ कुछ भी नहीं है, कुछ भी नहीं है, मैं ही हूं, ठीक है, यह सब की तरह दिखता है, हम कुछ ध्यान से शुरू करते हैं"

Everybody nodded their heads and closed their eyes and said: "Om" all together.

They chanted, meditated.

Before they knew it, 22 hours had passed.

Lunch was served: a single, triangular slice of yurple watermelon for each devotee.

They ate in unison, taking one bite, chewing it 22 times, then taking another, chewing it 22 times, and so on.

On the final bite, they exploded into mushroom clouds of yurple blood that disintegrated into an all-consuming brite wite lite, that then faded into a deep dark black.

With the deepest, darkest, blackest depth of the deep dark black, Mariposita flapped her amethyst wing and every eye in the universe blinked one cosmic blink, returning the devotees to the calm, breezy backyard lawn of The Yogi Zero Temple of the Yoga Azteca.

"What was that?" asked an anonymous burly devotee.

"The God Fish," answered Yogi Zero.

"Now," said Parahamsa Wind, "to the Isolation Chambers."

20. ISOLATION CHAMBERS

"Zen, Zen, Zen, Zen, Zen, Zen, Zen, Zen, Zen, Zen, Zen, Zen, Zen, Zen…"

Fausto was in his isolation chamber saying: "Zen, Zen, Zen, Zen, Zen, Zen, Zen, Zen, Zen, Zen, Zen, Zen, Zen…"

It was a nice feeling, isolation. Voluntary isolation, that

is. Involuntary isolation had the opposite effect. Fausto pondered that curious paradox, recalling his 666 years in solitary confinement in The Land of the Dead.

He shuffled through his pedestrian little emotions, anger, sadness, pain, reflection, wonder, hope, happiness, etc., until he had ran through all of them and was left with that big wide open emptiness, El Nada, the nothing/everything, the everything/everything, dem Aztec Yoga vibes, the big whatever whatever, the forever infinite internal cosmic universal dot, the Zig Zag Zig, pura alma, the soul's quietude reverberating through spacetime, the shimmering prismatic rainbow of existence, the throbbing gristle of life, the meta-joyous confetti of total awareness, the wriggling, undulating super duper maney wild exhilarating errythang, the zen zen zen zen zen zen zen zen zen zen zen zen zen zen, the wow, wow, the oh my god oh wow my god wow, the ceremonial flower song of the hungry coyote, the भाषा रूपक है, मेटा चार पांच है, पांच मनुष्य है, शक्ति, परिशोधन, पशु अपना भूत मानता है, शब्दों की कोई ज़रूरत नहीं, ध्वनि की कोई आवश्यकता नहीं, भाषा की कोई ज़रूरत नहीं, बुद्धि की आवश्यकता नहीं, महसूस करने की कोई आवश्यकता नहीं है , ज़रूरत के लिए कोई ज़रूरत नहीं, कोई ज़रूरत नहीं, कोई ज़रूरत नहीं, मेरे लिए कोई ज़रूरत नहीं, तुम्हारे लिए कोई ज़रूरत नहीं है, आप मुझे हैं, मैं हूं, हम हम हैं, कोई नहीं, हम यहाँ नहीं हैं , यहाँ नहीं है, वहां नहीं है, यहां है, कहीं नहीं है सब कुछ है, सब कुछ कुछ भी नहीं है, कुछ भी नहीं है, मैं ही हूं, ठीक है, यह सब की तरह दिखिता है, हम कुछ ध्यान से शुरू करते हैं, that Aztec Yoga, that flower tree, that Xiahuilompehua xiahuiloncuican ticuicanitl huiya ma xonahuiacany, onelelquixtilon ypalnemohuani. Yyeo ayahui ohuaya, Ma xonahuiacani ye techonquimiloa ypalnemohua ye xochimaquiztica netotilo ye nehuihuio-Aya!-moxochiuh-A ohuaya-yao yao ho ama y yehuaya ahuayyao aye ohuaya

ohuaya. Ye momamana, ye momana ya in tocuic. Maquiz-
calitec zan teocuitlacalico moyahuan Xochincuahuitl oo, Ye
mohui xohua in zan ye motzetzeloa. Ma in tlachichina quet-
zaltototl ma in tlachichina in zaquan quecholan. Ohuaya,
Xochincuahuitl timochiuh, timaxelihui, tihuitolihui: o ya
timoquetzaco in yehuan. Ixpan timomati tehuan nipapan
xochitl. A Ohuaya ohuaya, Ma oc xon ya tica oc xon cue-
pontica yn tlalticpac in. Timolinia tepehui xochitl, timot-
zetzeloa-Yohuaya ohuaya! Ah tlamiz noxochiuh ah tlamiz
nocuic yn noconyayehua-Aaya!-zan nicuicanitl. Huia. Xex-
elihuiya moyahua yaho cozahua ya xochitl za ye on calaqui-
lo zaquan calitic. A ohuaya ohuaya, Yn cacaloxochitl in
mayexochitl-Aya ohuaye!-tic ya moyahua, tic ya tzetzeloa
xochincalaytec. A ohuaya ohuaya, Yyoyahue ye nonocuil-
tonohua on nitepiltzin niNezahualcoyotl huia nic nechico
cozcatl in quetzalin patlahuac ye no nic iximati chalchihuitl.
Yaho in tepilhuan. Ohuaya ohuaya. Yxco nontlatlachia ne-
papan cuauhtli ocelotl, ye no nic yximati chalchiuhtliya in
maquiztliya. Ohuaye, Tiazque yehua xon ahuiacan. Niquit-
toa o ni Nezahualcoyotl. Huia! Cuix oc nelli nemohua oa in
tlalticpac? Yhui. Ohuaye, Annochipa tlalticpac. Zan achica
ye nican. Ohuaye ohuaye. Tel ca chalchihuitl no xamani, no
teocuitlatl in tlapani, no quetzalli poztequi. Yahui ohuaye.
Anochipa tlalticpac zan achica ye nican. Ohuaya ohuaya, ya
tu sabes…

And all of a sudden he blinked out of it, back to whatever silly little flesh realm theatre he'd conjured up in a butterfly dream.

"How long was I in there?" Fausto asked as he stepped
out of the isolation chamber, blinking in the brite wite lite
of the day.

"777 years," said Parahamsa Wind. Or did she? Maybe he was still in the Isolation chamber? There was no way
to tell anymore. Nor any real need. He was forever Fausto
Fausto regardless.

Fausto Fausto was on the Chatham Islands, awaiting repairs on the ship where he was working as a notary. While taking a walk through the lush tropical landscape, he happened upon a harsh, brutal, vulgar scene, a slavedriver was flogging a Moriori dude.

"Hey fucker, quit flogging that dude," Fausto said to the slavedriver.

"Mind your fuckin' business before I flog your ass too!"

"The fuck you just say to me?"

"I said mind your own fucking business before I flog your sorry mongrel ass too!"

So Fausto whupped his ass til he was out cold with his face leaking.

Moriori dude was like, "Good looks fam, but bruh finna go off when he wake up."

Fausto thought for a second and decided fuck it, took the six shooter off the slavedriver's belt, popped him in the head twice, took dude's sack o' gold coins, took a hand full for himself, tossed the rest to Moriori dude, found slavedriver dude's key ring, unshackled Moriori dude.

Moriori dude was like, "Goddamn, you a real one! I'm Autua Jr., what's your name?"

"Fausto."

"No doubt, no doubt."

"Aight, peace."

Fausto went up on his way and climbed an infamous local volcano by the name of Conicular Tor, jumped in, it was deeper than he had eyeballed and he had a kind of rough landing, got a lil scraped up, dusted himself off.

Down in the crater were hella faces carved up into trees.

The faces were wild strange and beautiful. Terrible, joyful, radiant, terrifying, glowing gems, horrifying, sexually outrageous, gratifying, mind-boggling, true works of nasty brute aesthetic strength and power, highly potent facial images, prismatic, magnanimous in nature, truly, buckwild, a delight, a wonder to behold, these things was flamey, sick, saucy, pretty ass art. So why the fuck were they in this crater? Who knew? Who cared? Not Fausto.

He peaced from the crater, made his way back to the ship, which looked to be all cranked up and ready to set sail again, hopped aboard like "Sayonara, suckers" to nobody in particular, casted off.

On the ship, Fausto's homie Dr. Goose Goose was like: "Hey dude, you look all banged up."

"Yeah, I jumped in a volcano, think i sustained some injuries from that lil stunt."

"Well, let me examine you then."

"Word, word, might as well let you know I got this other lil chronic ailment too."

"Word, word, I'ma do a whole physical, pause."

They headed to the sick bay for a lil check up.

"Hmm... interesting."

"What's up doc?"

"Looks like you got yourself a fatal parasite, I'ma get you on some pills," He pulled out a bottle: "Take two of these lil puppies a day till the bottle's empty."

"No doubt."

Fausto went back to his cabin, and who was there but Autua Jr.

"How'd you get in here?"

"Snuck in."

"Damn."

"Let me get a job on this ship till we get to Hava'ii."

"Hold up let me ask the captain."

They went to Captain Ducko, a mellow guy; he gave

Autua Jr. a job tying ropes and shit. "But there's no more cabins left so you got bunk up with Fausto, here you can make a hammock out of these tater sacks."

They went back to the cabin, Fausto threw Autua Jr. a comic book and a candy bar and fell asleep.

The sun set over the Pacific and the ship sailed on into the night.

22. BANANA TEMPURA

Fausto was at Agrabah Bail Bonds in South Deadstown bailing out Chuck who'd got hemmed up in the Land of the Dead.

The office was ugly, all offices are, but this one archetypally so. Fausto hated offices. Offices are pure evil, of the most banal type. He handed over some dead coins to the skeleton bondsman and signed some dead paper with a dead blackbird blood ink-filled dead skeleton finger pen.

He went outside and smoked a cigarette. Fuckin' Land of the Dead. Some picturesque lonely vistas, but the bureaucracy was brutal.

When he came back, the skeleton bondsman was just getting off the phone. "Go wait outside the dead pig station across the street, they'll let him out in about an hour."

"Wow that was quick."

"You got lucky this time."

Fausto went over to a dead Japanese restaurant called 死んだ皇帝 and had a couple dead beers to kill some time. The waitress brought him some banana tempura with a scoop of vanilla coconut milk ice cream, "On the house."

"Thanks toots."

He took a bite. It was the best banana tempura he'd

ever had. He wasn't a big dessert guy either. But this banana tempura was crazy, it felt like butterfly sex.

He walked back over to the dead pig station and smoked another ciggy waiting for Chuck. After some time, Chuck emerged.

"You look like shit."

"So do you."

They went to get some dead beers at 死んだ皇帝 and Fausto ordered two more banana tempuras, one for him and one for Chuck.

"I don't want no banana tempura," Chuck said.

"Just try it."

"Naw, I'll just try a bite of yours."

"Hell naw, I'm eating mine."

"Dog, I don't even want none anyway."

"You will."

"Naw, dude."

"I'ma order it anyway, take one bite, if you don't like it, I'll take yours too."

"Whatever dude."

Their plates came out. Chuck took a bite.

"Damn this is the best fuckin banana tempura I ever had."

"That's what I said."

"And I'm not even a dessert guy."

"Me neither."

They moved on to some dead sake, first hot, 111 bottles, then cold, another 111 bottles, then another 111 bottles of hot again.

By the time they left they were pretty loaded.

"I'm going to the dead titty bar," said Chuck.

"I'ma just get a cheap dead motel room and pass out."

"A'ight then, peace."

"Peace."

23. GHOST DOG

Fausto woke up in a shitty dead motel in South Deadstown.

There was a knock on the door.

"Go away."

"Fausto!"

"Dead Louie?"

He went to the door.

"Dead Louie. The fuck are you doing here? How'd you know I was here?"

"I got a lot of eyes in Deadstown, Faustino, I keep track of my people."

Dead Louie was in the import-export business, he had a lot of connections, he had saved Fausto's life a few years back when some unsavory characters were upset about a gambling debt. Fausto still owed him one.

"You still owe me one."

"I know."

"I know how you can pay me back."

Fausto yawned, "How?"

Dead Louie handed him a dead six shooter.

"Naw man, that's not really my line of work. I don't like those things, too loud."

"I'm not asking you, I'm telling you. You owe me your life. Besides the guy's dead already, I just need you to send him to the Land of the Double Dead."

Fausto stood there thinking about it. Dead Louie put the dead gun in his hand.

"Like I said, I'm not asking."

"Who is he?"

"Handsome Frank Skeleton. He's sleeping with Devil Don Vargo's daughter Daisy, and the old man wants him out of the picture."

Dead Louie handed Fausto a scrap of paper with the address:

2377 Magnolia Blvd.North Deadstown, Land of the Dead

Fancy neighborhood.

Fausto memorized the address and burned the scrap of paper in the ashtray.

"Here's the key to the brown Buick outside, just park it here when you're done, unlocked with the key in the glove, I'll have somebody pick it up. And here's something for your troubles."

A couple stacks of dead dollars wrapped in dead rubber bands. Then Dead Louie was gone.

Fausto took a shower, watched some TV, smoked a cigarette, then drove up to North Deadstown.

He parked outside the house and waited for the poor sucker to come out. He dozed off for a second, woke up to the sound of a car door slamming, saw that Handsome Frank Skeleton had gotten into his Cadillac. Damn. He tailed him. They headed south.

Dude ended up parking in a motel not but three blocks from Fausto's motel.

Fausto waited for Handsome Frank Skeleton to get inside his room then went and knocked on his door.

BANG. BANG.

Simple as that.

But wait, footsteps.

Daisy came out the bathroom:

"What the fuck?"

Fausto said nothing.

Daisy walked over to the bedside table, picked up a book, handed it to Fausto, "Now get the fuck out of here," she said.

Fausto bounced.

Decided to head to Vegas for a couple days.

Fausto was posted up in a suite at the Casino Paradiza Infiniti in Las Vegas. They knew him here, had a reputation for being something of a whale, he'd won big a few times and was a generous tipper, got to know the dealers and managers.

He wrote a brief letter to Mariposita on a Casino Paradiza Infiniti postcard:

Amor,

Hiding out for a bit. See u real soon te prometo.

F

He rolled the card up into a cigarillo-width scroll, dropped it into a glass vial, corked the vial, tied it to the foot of a pigeon he sent flying out the window, popped a couple pills and drank some whiskey while watching TV, trying to figure out what was next.

He looked at the book Daisy had handed him.

PEYOTE KARAOKE

He knew the book. His father had written it but he'd always been told it had never been released, only a few galley copies, sent out to various publishing houses, agents, critics, etc.

He'd never read it. His father had told him long ago it was garbage, drivel, pura basura. He took his father at his word.

He felt an impending sense of doom, the creeping of death's hand from around some corner of the future.

He rolled a joint and smoked some weed, watched some TV: The Island of Death.

He hated this show but kept watching.

It was him, Fausto Fausto, on the screen.

He walked to a wooden table with a glass jar of distilled holy water and two sunflowers in it.

He sat in the chair.

There was a chair opposite of him.

From stage left walked Fausto Fausto, who sat in the other chair.

They sat facing each other: Fausto Fausto & Fausto Fausto.

A third Fausto Fausto in a tuxedo entered the frame holding a plate in each hand, each plate holding a triangular slice of watermelon.

Fausto Fausto placed the watermelon slices in front of Fausto Fausto and Fausto Fausto.

Fausto Fausto and Fausto Fausto ate their respective watermelon slices.

Fausto flipped the channel: The Bernie Mac Show, he'd seen this one.

He flipped the channel again:

PEYOTE KARAOKE...

It was the opening credits to the film adaptation of his father's book.

Fausto put the remote down, hit the whiskey and started rolling a joint.

The movie opened on an uncomfortably long and quiet shot of a regal mansion in a picturesque European countryside, late afternoon on a sunny, yet crisp, cloud-speckled, late winterish, early springish day.

A subtitle eventually appeared:

Zedelgem, Belgium, 1931.

Next, an equally uncomfortably long and quiet shot of the large front door of the mansion.

After 33 minutes of this door, another subtitle appeared. Fausto had smoked three joints by this point and was finally stoned enough to feel like reading a subtitle. It read:

The Mansion of The Barron Maestro Ludwig Rainier Maria Von Trilke.

Fausto popped a pill, hit the whiskey and started rolling another joint.

After about 333 minutes of this new subtitle floating

like an iceberg in the arctic sea of this dark forest green door, almost black, a deep green that became blue and purple on deep and thorough examination, there was finally another cut, it felt violent, aggressive, almost unnecessary.

We were now in the chamber, a silhouette shot of a man at a desk writing on a parchment with a quill and ink.

This shot held for 33 hours.

And then, like a bolt of beautiful lightning, another subtitle:

The Chamber of Fausto Fausto.

This shot held for another 33 hours.

Cut to Fausto Fausto's hand as he dragged the ink-dipped feather across the parchment, overlaid in dissolve with a panning shot of the letter he was writing, written large and in full, so the words could be clearly read, Fausto Fausto narrating in voiceover:

Dear Mariposita,

I have found myself in the chamber of a rather regal old mansion in the countryside of Zedelgem, near Bruges, under the employ of the reclusive virtuoso Barron Maestro Ludwig Rainier Maria Von Trilke, as an amanuensis, tasked with transcribing the final stages of what he hopes to be his Magnum Opus, The Trillepathy for Several Seasons, the Devil's Repose in the Angel's Desert Campground; Sonata in Q Diagonal Majorus-Metti-Minorus, which he sometimes refers to casually as Der Todtenvogel. The Barron Maestro suffers from no physical, mental, or emotional disease that I'm aware of, yet he insists he suffers from a "spiritual disease" (his words, not mine) that prohibits him from touching "any instrument, be it musical or otherwise, for the purposes of transcribing music" (again, his words) and so my labor consists of notating the melodies he hums, sings, and whistles to me at his whim, as we order and shape the various movements to his liking. He is an eccentric, that is to be sure, but the music is thoroughly emotionally articulate. I am learning a great deal. It has been a long, cold, bitter winter, filled with long lamplit nights of composing and writing, wrestling with melodies and harmonies, fugues and counter fugues, swells, choruses, preludes, interludes, denouements and the like, but the work has finally turned a corner and fallen into place, and I believe it will live up to all expectations. I suspect we shall finish by the end of the month with plenty of time to prepare the orchestra for the premiere this summer. Alas, I hear the bell beckoning me to his drawing room, more work awaits me, I will write again at another time.

Sincerely,Fausto

Cut to the luxurious west wing drawing room of the reclusive virtuoso Barron Maestro Ludwig Rainier Maria Von Trilke, crisp late winter, early spring sunlight streaming in through the parted white linen curtains of the looming windows, alighting deep dark stained oak floors adorned with deep burgundy and dark black forest green velvet and tables dressed in white lace, a fire crackling in the grand marble fireplace in anticipation of the impending chill of dusk, a grand piano in the center of the room, a desk beside it, sheets of music notation sitting in a handful of small piles, a quill resting in an ink jar, and beside the desk, a small but impeccably elegant lounging divan upholstered in green velvet.

Barron Maestro Ludwig Rainier Maria Von Trilke paced the room in silhouette, backlit by the towering windows, humming vigorously, gesticulating wildly with his arms like a mother heron protecting her nest.

The shot is held for 333 hours.

During this time, Fausto called up room service and ordered more whiskey and some popcorn, drank a glass of water, rolled another joint, room service came, Fausto ate the popcorn and drank the whiskey and smoked 999 joints, ordering more whiskey and drinking that, then ordering more whiskey.

Finally a subtitle appeared:

The West Wing Drawing Room of Barron Maestro Ludwig Rainier Maria Von Trilke

The subtitle held for another 333 hours, then disappeared as Fausto Fausto entered screen right. Upon seeing him, Herr Ludwig walked into the firelight and it became evident that he was also played by Fausto Fausto.

He nodded to Fausto and continued to hum and gesticulate as Fausto sat at the piano, immediately starting to pick out the notes of the melody and the chords behind them.

After 666 hours of this, seven butlers, Fausto Fausto, Fausto Fausto, Fausto Fausto, Fausto Fausto, Fausto Fausto, Fausto Fausto, and Fausto Fausto walked into the drawing room holding a wooden table, two wooden chairs, a Ming Dynasty Chinese vase filled with holy water holding two yellow roses, and two plates each containing a single triangular slice of watermelon. They set the table and filed out of the room.

Fausto Fausto and Barron Maestro Ludwig Rainier Maria Von Trilke (played by Fausto Fausto, using split screen technology), rose from their work and sat at the table, eating the watermelon slices in perfect unison, exploding into twin mushroom clouds of blood, the blood dissolving into a hyper pink mist, the mist swirling ad infinitum.

"Perfect," said Barron Maestro Ludwig Rainier Maria Von Trilke, "We've finished ahead of schedule."

25. FAYAMANZANEM

Act 2 of PEYOTE KARAOKE opened again on Fausto Fausto writing a letter to his dear Mariposita:

Dear Mariposita,

After countless arduous rehearsals, the Zedelgem Philharmonic Orchestra finally debuted The Trillepathy for Several Seasons, the Devil's Repose in the Angel's Desert Campground; Sonata in Q Diagonal Majorus-Metti-Minorus at the Vyvyan Ayrs Memorial Concert Hall. We were received with thunderous applause and the critics praised the work as an inimitable and immortal masterpiece. It now plays nightly in Krakow, I supervised the first week of performances and then returned with the maestro to his estate where we are now at work on another 444 movements, a sequel. The work is slow-going but by and by, it is beginning to take shape. Anyway, I must be going now, the Barron Maestro has graciously extended an invitation for me to dine with him and his wife the good Lady Farfalla, Arch-Duchess of Corsica. In all of the months I have been under the employ of the Barron Maestro he has never extended an invitation to dine with him and his wife. Indeed, I have never even caught a glimpse of her in the vast and sprawling hallways and gardens of his estate. I was beginning to suspect she was a figment of his imagination. I am expected to be seated in the grand salle a manger at Seventeen-and-Five-and-a-Half-Sixths-of-the-Hour sharp, I must wash up and don my finest suit. I will write again at another time.

Sincerely,Fausto

Cut to the extravagant grand dining hall, the Barron Maestro seated at the head of a lavishly set 100-foot long dining table, Fausto seated at the foot.

"Forgive me for asking Herr Maestro, but where is your wife?" asked Fausto. "I was looking forward to finally making her acquaintance."

"What was that?" shouted the Barron Maestro, his voice echoing through the high ceilinged dining room.

The head butler, Fausto Fausto, walked from his post

by the kitchen door to whisper Fausto's question into the Maestro's ear.

The Maestro, in lieu of a verbal response, lifted his index finger and onto it flitted an amethyst butterfly. The butterfly was Mariposita.

Cut to a 333 year close up of Fausto's face, frozen in shock and confusion.

Fausto sat in his Paradiza Infiniti suite for 333 years watching the scene with the exact same frozen look of shock and confusion.

Finally a cut, to Fausto, back in his chamber after dinner, laying in his bed with the same frozen look of shock and confusion.

The door opened softly. In flitted Mariposita. Without a word, they made intense butterfly love, after which Fausto fell into a deep sleep as Mariposita silently flitted back out of the room.

Fausto, in his Paradiza Infiniti suite, also fell asleep. And when he awoke, the film was long over and another episode of Island of Death was on the TV. He turned off the TV, picked up the copy of Peyote Karaoke that Daisy Vargo had given him, and cracked it open.

26. STILL AT IT

The book bore little to no significant resemblance to the movie:

CHAPTER ONE: FREE EVERYBODY

I was at the Hilton in Miami, drunk, stoned, high off speed, watching TV. The TV was watching me too.

My name is LL Cool J and I'm a famous professional rapper.

America's Saddest Girl was on, twelve sexy females were weeping.

I changed the channel, Hitler doc.

I changed the channel, Law & Order.

Changed the channel, Miami Vice.

Changed the channel, Miami Vice, the movie.

Changed the channel, it was the VH1: Behind the Music of me. I watched for a bit.

I rolled a blunt and lit it, flipped some more channels. Dubs beat the Cavs.

I had half a pitcher of mimosa left from brunch, still cold to the touch. I poured a mimosa and then tipped the contents of an MDMA gel cap into it.

Flipped the channel: Fieri.

Fieri was making sausage with a plump white lady and I was jamming hard going Nirvana.

The TV was humming and glowing. The TV started to bleed.

I ordered a six shooter from room service.

Juan (his name tag said Juan — who knows how he self identified for real for real, maybe as Juan, maybe not. Maybe he was LL Cool J. Who am I, LL Cool J, to say?) brought the gun up on a pillow. I tipped him twenty and shot him, as is the custom in the United States.

I jumped out the window and landed on a crocodile and rode the crocodile around like a skateboard.

I stopped into a store and bought a Miami Dolphins snapback. The hat was like a shark fin.

When I left the store my crocodile was nowhere to be found.

I bought an empanada, chicken flavor.

The sky was a beautiful pink.

I caught a cab to the beach and swam to Cuba, visited my old pal Fidel Castro. We caught up on thangs. He had on an Adidas brand tracksuit as per usualmente. We smoked cigars and talked about baseball, the Cubs had just won the World Series for the first time in literally over a hundred years. We ruminated on that.

I caught a first class flight back to Miami. I told the lady at the front desk I'd like to stay permanently in my room. She slipped me a business card with her phone number written on the back. I memorized the number and destroyed it. You can never be too careful.

A tropical rain storm started instantly as soon as I returned to my room. Thunder was cracking ferociously. Lightning struck the palm tree outside my window and a coconut fell onto my balcony and cracked in half. I have been told this is an auspicious sign.

I sat down immediately to write my memoirs:

"When I'm alone in my room, sometimes I stare at the wall."

That was enough for today.

Fausto shut the book. Whoever adapted the screenplay appeared to have taken a lot of liberties. He showered and took the elevator down to the casino floor to shoot some dice.

27. DOLFINISMO

Down on the floor, Fausto's hand was hot. He'd had plenty of unlucky days, but when he was on he was on, when the luck arrived, it was supernatural, he had a whole table of side bettors going off, the drink was flowing, the room took on a rosy winning glow.

It began to feel too intense and when Fausto sensed a swift turn of luck approaching, he bowed out, to the protest of everyone around him. He went back to his suite to take a soak in the pool on the balcony.

When he made it back to his suite, he noticed right

away something was amiss. His eyes zeroed in on the bedside table where he distinctly remembered leaving his copy of Peyote Karaoke, but the book was not there. He searched the whole suite and it was nowhere to be found, nothing else was out of place. His money was still locked in his safe, he threw it in the money counter again to make sure, nothing was missing.

He showered and threw on his trunks, went out and jumped in the pool. He swam 777 laps, breaststroke, then lay in the sun, thinking.

The missing book was ominous no question, but merely lit up the familiar sublime paranoia of the whole violent opera. There was a loose handfuls of yin yangs he'd yet to spiritually unknot. In a more pragmatic light he pondered some realities: not only did Daisy have her own goons she could set on his head (although a strange, irrational intuition was telling him this situation was unlikely), Handsome Frank Skeleton — who, while not a capo, had juice, ambitions, and a generous sprinkling of mean friends of all stripes and was, perhaps most significantly, lieutenant to some heavy hitters in the Skeletino Family — would also likely want revenge. On top of that, the Skeletinos were politically cozy with some of the brass in the Dead Vargos, giving Dead Don Vargo — the boss himself, whose leadership was sliding, who was growing paranoid, who suspected some turncoats in his midst, who might have even been fearing retribution from his own daughter — more than a few reasons to not want any loose ends that could implicate him in the murder of Handsome Frank Skeleton. Gone were the days when Dead Don Vargo could kill with impunity, protected by the aura of fear associated with his name and an army of loyal heads and hitters backing him without question; he was an old man now and there were wolves in the throne room, and he, being an old wolf himself, was prone to snap on anybody. A messy situation.

So why had Dead Don Vargo ordered the hit in the first place? Louie hadn't really offered much of an explanation, and whatever explanation he'd have offered under questioning would've been mere puppetry or else shallow conjecture. Only the Don knew his true motives. And then, probably not even him. It seems like mayhaps it was a sort of impressionistic melange of conflicting ideas, the unavoidable irrationality of human logic and its ugly mechinations, that gassed the Dead Don's foggy evil heart engine. Maybe he thought the hit would give him some leverage, get an annoying young upstart out of the way and keep the Skeletinos from further encroaching on his familial holdings. Maybe underestimated the complexity of the stakes. Sure, Handsome Frank Skeleton was no saint, and there were no shortage of would-be culprits with no shortage of motives, Don Vargo had likely been banking on a clean, quiet execution, at most inciting a minor skirmish that ended with some foot soldiers dead and everyone moving on. In retrospect, the wishful thinking of the plan felt evident. The fatalistic nihilism (nihilist fatalism? who cares) of an old mean fucker with not one fuck left to give, perhaps never even had one.

Fausto figured his best option, just to be on the safe side, was to kill the entire Dead Vargo Family. At least in the Land of the Double Dead, they could carry on their business with fewer tax restrictions and less police interference. Then Double Dead Don Vargo and Dead Handsome Frank Skeleton could settle their score out there, mano-a-mano for all he cared.

He swam 111 more laps, backstroke, then showered, dressed, cleaned his pistol and loaded it with 666 bullets, took the elevator down to the parking lot, and hopped on his Harley to The Land of the Dead.

Fausto buzzed into New Death City on his 11996677 Harley Love Electric, stopped at a little hipster bar in North Deathfield called Flames of Hell.

He ordered a Dead Skeleton Bourbon on the rocks and watched the dead baseball game.

The Dead Devils were beating the Dead Angels.

Dead Curtis came in, they shot some pool, Fausto won 555 dead bucks. Dead Curtis said double or nothing, Fausto said plus a buck, Dead Curtis was like fsho, Fausto came up 1111 dead bucks now, he hit a perfect streak after his break and doubled up within minutes. Curtis said let's go again, Fausto went around the world on the guy, it was a robbery simple and plain and the guy was liking it the whole time, Fausto kept wondering what the hustle was, waiting for the bite but it never came. He ended up with D$999,999,999.99 when Dead Curtis finally bowed out. It was like a temple offering, a charitable donation.

Dead Curtis lit a cigarette, lent one to Fausto.

"Say, Dead Curtis..."

"Yeah?"

"What's it like being dead?"

"You should know."

"Good game, man."

"Not for me."

Curtis drew but Fausto drew faster and shot him dead.

"Et tu, Curtis?"

As Curtis's dead body smoked, Fausto took his leave while the saloon patrons scratched their head at the curious scene that'd transpired.

Fausto hopped on his Love Electric and zipped over to Don Vargo's mansion, killed everyone there, spared Daisy, then galloped on over to Tino Skeletino's mansion, laid them to waste, then swam over to Gino Skeletino's mansion, cleaned up house there as well.

He checked his pistol, one bullet left.

The last bullet he dipped in watermelon sugar and swallowed like a pill, woke up in Chapter 29.

29. AWAITING THE SPLENDOR
(IN WATERMELON SUGAR)

Fausto awoke for the infinite-th time from his Never-Ending Isolation Chamber Session at The Yogi Zero Temple of the Yoga Azteca and Subsidiary Arts, Sciences & Philosophies, he felt mildly vortextual, unsure of how long he had been in there, if anything was real, etc. Who cared? Here he was at the The Yogi Zero Temple of the Yoga Azteca and Subsidiary Arts, Sciences & Philosophies, diving within himself trying to find La Pura Magica de La Yoga Azteca.

They hit up the lawn again for more chants and prayers, fruit salad, then they lazed around in the grass, chillin, watching the clouds pass overhead, all in various states of casual meditation.

Fausto was chilling on the grass, Mariposita asleep on his nose, when a familiar lookin' dude came up to him.

"What up Fausto."

"Sup…"

"It's your boy KOOL A.D."

"Oh hey what up fam," Fausto pretended he knew who that was.

"Look, man, I don't have much time, take this."

It was a CD in a clear plastic case. The CD was silver, the words AZTEC YOGA written in black.

"What's this?"

"My latest mixtape, it's fire, give it a listen."

And just like that, KOOL A.D. was gone.

Mariposita woke up.

"What happened?"

"Iono."

"Wuzat."

"CD"

"What's on it?"

"Aztec Yoga. It's KOOL A.D.'s new mixtape, apparently it's fire."

"Where you get it."

"From KOOL A.D."

"Where he go?"

"Iono."

"Let's go listen to it."

"O.K."

They went back to their casita, threw it on the boombox. It slapped. Puro fuego, all bars, peak bars, it moved the culture forward, they got stoned and made sweet groovy butterfly love.

The bell rang for some more meditation or whatever, they took a nap instead, woke up at the break of dusk, wandered the grounds, found their way to a place they'd never seen before, dense trees, a dizzying hedge maze, a country stone wall, they hopped over it, an Ivy-draped brick wall, a big ass plum tree leaning lazily against it. They climbed the plum tree, ate some plums and jumped over to the other side, more garden stuff, flowers and whatnot, then a long uphill slope of grass, followed by a long downward slope of grass, a couple more of those and finally a stretch of cement, a steel grated trench with various drainage and ventilation pipes, another stretch of cement and chainlink fence with barbed wire around it. Beyond that, what looked like the warehouse district of a long abandoned American City of Industry, presumably the warehouse district of some suburb of Los Discos.

They found a hole in the fence and crawled through, wandered the warehouses overgrown with grass, moss, ferns and whatever.

They popped into a massive, seemingly endless hangar, with its three-story gates flung wide open. It was filled with knick knacks, curios, memorabilia, various miscellania, artifacts, antiques, paintings, sculptures, musical instruments, furniture, boxes, tubs, urns, shelves, and crates of books, comics, magazines, pamphlets, records, CDs, cassette tapes, Laser Discs, DVDs, VHS tapes, beta tapes, Blu Ray Discs, external hard drives, MP3 players, toys, balloons, party decorations, chandeliers, bicycles, cases of photographs, coin collections, butterfly collections (Mariposita shuddered), stamp collections, beetle collections, precious gem collections, bottles, cans, jars, weapons, artillery, cooking equipment, automotive equipment, cars, trucks, planes, boats, tanks, helicopters, hardware, toys, mannequins, maps, globes, stereo equipment, household appliances, canned and other nonperishable food items, beauty products, liquors, cigarettes, controlled substances, pornography, jewelry, piles of money of all currencies, racks of clothing of all styles, costumes, masks, etc., etc., everything in abundance, in various stages of wear and tear, much of it brand new, and beyond all that, various well-watered, well-kept plants, edible, decorative, shade-providing, etc., and beyond that, a vast, intricate silk Persian rug, with a lush leather and mahogany living room set up, nine tigers seated on various sofas, divans, loveseats, chairs, pillows, one of them in a hammock.

They had some Psychedelic Tiger Music playing on an old but well-cared-for record player. The sounds were beautiful, they were smoking shisha with hashish and opium, luxuriating.

In the center of their little living room spread was a big clay chimenea with a pine fire going, some palo santo, sandalwood, sage, and copal thrown on there, sprinkled with jasmine and rose oils, making for a bewitching scent.

"Sup y'all," said Fausto to a scattered, casual rejoindering of sups.

"Have a seat, hit this shisha."

Fausto and Mariposita sat and commenced to zoot, lounge.

"Where do y'all come from?" asked one of the tigers, a girl.

"The Yogi Zero Temple of the Yoga Azteca and Subsidiary Arts, Sciences & Philosophies," said Mariposita.

"How'd I guess," she said to herself as she blew smoke rings, looking off.

"We finna run up in there and rob the place," said another Tiger.

"Shut up Joey, why you tell em that?"

"Don't matter," said Joey, "they couldn't stop us even if they wanted to."

"Hey, I got an idea," said the tigress that had been blowing smoke rings, "Team up with us."

All the tigers laughed.

"We're just busting your balls," said the smoke ring tigress, "I'm Tina."

"Sup, Tina,"

"Sup, Tina."

They all sat smoking, vibing out to the Psychedelic Tiger Music. Crazy stuff.

When the record ended, one of the tiger's threw on KOOL A.D.'s new mixtape AZTEC YOGA, it was fire flames, wall-to-wall slappers, the vibes were through the roof, real wavy stuff, preemo beats, hi quality bars.

30. PURO RAP JUGO

"What was that last one called?" asked Fausto.

"Awaiting the Splendor," said DJ Vikram, the tiger who'd been manning the record player.

"And what's this one called?"

"Puro Rap Jugo."

It was a story rap, it took place in Nuevas Buenas Yerbas, Nueva California, in the year 7777. The protagonist, Luisa Del Rey, by a chance encounter in a stalled elevator, came to befriend a man named Rufio Sexo. They remained trapped in the elevator for 33 days and over this time began to open up to each other, tell their life stories, eventually fall in love and proceed to make love constantly until finally being rescued from themselves. During the courting stage, Luisa told Rufio that she was a journalist and that her father, now dead, was an "incorruptible" policeman before gaining some notoriety as a war correspondent, and Rufio let slip that the Meta-Nuclear Power Plant where he worked, El Diamante Negro, was emanating powerful radiations known as Meta-Nuclear Zig Zag Waves that were distorting the very fabric of reality. Thirty-three days after they were rescued from the elevator, Rufio was found dead in what was ruled a suicide. Although Luisa and Rufio had fallen hard for each other in that stalled elevator, once they were freed, the love seemed to evaporate, they exchanged numbers, more out of a mutual sense of obligation than anything else, went to their respective apartments, and met up on a couple occasions for casual sex until they eventually stopped contacting each other. When Luisa read about Rufio "committing suicide" in the Nuevas Buenas Yerbas Daily Fake News, she felt an oscillatory cocktail of sadness, fear, terror, rage, numb detachment, confusion, half-bemusement, shock, and curiosity in varying combination and ended up wondering who, specifically, had killed him, what they looked like, how they dressed the scene afterwards, where they lived, what they did that night, the next morning, what they had eaten, etc. Being an investigative reporter by trade, employed by Absolute State Media Corporation (affectionately referred to as A.S.M.C.), the largest Fake News corporation in the Mysterion Hemisphere, owned by OMNICORP (the national corporation of the Nea Nea So So Copros Copros hyper corporate fascistic state who had, it turned out, recently acquired El Diamante Negro in a hostile takeover), she put her investigative reporting skills (along with her booty call key) to work, gaining access to Rufio's home, where she collected every piece of information about the Meta-Nuclear Zig Zag Waves Radiations of El Diamante Negro, then gaining access to his work files from his coworker/simpatico Bo China, whose plane to Las Ramblas the following day mysteriously exploded. She feared that she was next. And she was right; on the long highway to Gran Burbuja, where she'd decided to hide out while the heat died down, she was run off the road by an agent of OMNICORP.

An incredibly intense song. The beat slapped tho.

"What's beyond this little warehouse district?" asked Mariposita.

"Well, you came from Aztec Yoga which is to the West," said Tina, "and to the North there's Bijouvia, to the east there's Jing De, and to the south there's Novo Ndoto."

"I want to check all those places out," said Mariposita.

"O.K.," said Joey, "I'll lend y'all one of the whips."

31. GODARD BURNER

Fausto and Mariposita whipped a leopard paint 196688 Peugeot 555-5-5-5 through the mellow Bijouvian countryside, waving their gleaming silver Smif & Wessider six shooters in the air, clapping into the cottony clouds, felling low-swooping doves that fell into the baskets of handkerchief-headed old village women, who waved and blew kisses. The trees swung past in a hazy gray Eurozoetropical blur, like skeletons sprinting to the Land of the Dead. Zoovielike, they blitted across the campos of Bijouvia, phantasmagoria varia seeping from the hollows of gnarled woody stumps, loraxical, nostalgically bemoaning the slaughter of their upper stems harvested and fused with orc into quixotical wind catchers, spinning the wheels of progress ever in the same circle, the mobius filmstrip of the rolling landscape's mind's eyeballs looping the infinite sorrows of earth's pedestrian societal dramas.

"La vie est un reve."

"La paix est la réalité."

"Le loyer est un vol."

"L'argent est une blague."

"La vérité est relative."

"Jouer est le travail le plus réel."

"La tristesse est une perte de temps."

"Le bonheur est la plus grande tristesse."

"Ecouter c'est parler."

"Parler est de chanter."

"Combien d'os le jour a-t-il eu?"

"Combien de dents la nuit a-t-elle?"

"Les dents sont les os."

"Les dents sont les graines de la fleur de la mort."

"La fleur de la mort est une simple larme dans l'œil de l'univers."

"L'univers est un canard dormant."

"Le sommeil est le cousin de la mort."

"La connaisance est une action, pas un objet."

"Le mensonges sont de belles vérités fausses."

"Quoi?"

"Ça ne fait rien."

They pulled the car over and made butterfly love in a grassy field, then lay there, smoking cigarettes, looking up into the cloudy gray-white sky.

Fausto and Mariposita whipped through downtown Luoti Nuyen, the capital of Jing De, looking for a mellow restaurant to luxuriate at.

"That one looks as good as any," said Mariposita, pointing to a spot called 李子.

"Cool, OK," said Fausto. He pulled over.

They walked in and were immediately led upstairs to an empty corner by a large window overlooking the huge bustling downtown sprawl, it was magnificent.

They ordered the Buddha's Garden, a vegetable tofu stir fry served over steamed rice that was supposed to be "amazing" here, according to the waiter donning an immaculate black silk changshan with matching black silk pants and slippers.

He brought out some tea and they sipped on that, smoking hash spliffs and zoning out to the Teng "Tina Tiger" Li-Chun songs playing out the warm vintagey speakers.

Their Buddha's Garden came and they had that, smoked more hash spliffs and zoned out to Teng "Tina Tiger" Li-Chun some more. Tina Tiger's Number One Mega Hit, "The Moon Is The Metaphorical Language Of My Heart," started.

"I love this one."

They listened for 777 hours, it was a long ass song.

They smoked 7,777 hash spliffs and zoned dreamily to the music.

The words translated more or less as such:

Money Is The Original Concept Of ManEvil Is IrrelevantThe True Nature of Your Being Is PeaceArrange Yourself As LoveA Breeze Through An Open WindowReality Has Made Itself ApparentWe Are FragileAt The End Our RopesThe Ends of The EarthThe Ocean Whispers A Song

To The MoonThe Moon Is The Metaphorical Language Of
My Heart

It was just that verse, repeated hundreds of thousands
of times, slight changes in melody, harmony, chord progres-
sion, rhythm section arrangement, key changes, solos, and
other musical bridges. Somehow it never got boring.

If he were to force a description of his feelings, throughout listening to the song, Fausto would probably have supplied: La Magica. Mariposita would likely have supplied
those same two words.

They turned their gaze from the spectacular view of
downtown Luoti Nuyen glowing just outside the window
and glanced over at the full length mirror on the opposite
wall to examine themselves in full, the city glittering like
jewelry behind them.

They looked slightly crazed yet beautiful, a mellow couple radiating joy.

At the end of the song, the impeccably dressed waiter
brought out two triangular watermelon slices in porcelain
bowls glazed in the classic blue and white Qingchan Dynasty era style, a temple scene in the mountains, nuns and
monks hoeing the fields.

They ate their watermelon slices with chopsticks and
exploded into twin mushroom clouds of blood, evaporating
into pure white and then pure black.

33. TOTAL RELEVANCE

They woke up in Novo Ndoto, in a palm-thatched-roof-hut
style cabin on a black sand beach at a luxury resort in Novo
Wimbo, a quiet vacationer's town tucked away on the South
Westernly coastline, overlooking The Pax Kusini Ocean.

The ocean shushed, magnifica.

The sun shot off rounds of hot light, shell-shocking the day into blinking existence.

Fausto and Mariposita stripped and ran through the perfect black sand into the perfect, wine-dark, deep blue ocean, let the waves carry them around, for a bit, laid in the sand for a while and jumped back in the water.

They did this for 77 hours, occasionally dipping back into the cabin to shower and fuck and then running back to the beach, the sun setting and rising a handful of times, only watermelon and champagne being consumed throughout.

By the end of their little vacation they were stained a deep dark blue, the same color as the ocean. The people of Novo Wimbo called this a "sea tan" and it only happened to those whose hearts were open to beauties of the highest vibrations.

They motored up the South Westerly Novo Ndoto coast admiring a brilliant sunset and then scraped right on into the vast, thick, rainforest interior of the country, massive trees vibrating with frogs, monkeys, beetles, spiders, snakes, parrots, fruit bats, dragonflies, butterflies, etc. while leopards, tapirs, elephants, tigers, etc. roamed the shady canopied jungle floors, punctuated by various streams and rivers. They stopped at a gas station next to a bridge over a quaint lil stream and filled up, bought a couple young coconuts, bruh macheted them open and they sipped the sweet water while gazing at the stream.

"It's beautiful out here," said Mariposita.

"Hella pretty yeah."

The jungle was squawkin and hummin, buzzin and flappin, hissin, cricketin, and whoopin and howlin, warblin, twitterin, tweetin, snortin, shushin, etc., a real spectacular tropical orchestra.

"Onde você está indo, familia?" said the gas station attendant that had macheted open their young cocos.

"Norte," replied Fausto.

"Pais Tigre."

"Si."

"Cuidado até lá."

"Sem dúvida."

They scraped off.

34. FRACTALS

As they pulled into the Tiger Hangar up in pais tigre, the homies Joey Tiger, Tina Tiger, DJ Vikram Tiger, and a few other tigers they hadn't met before greeted them by firing their AK-777s into the air.

"Sup y'all, how was the honeymoon?"

"Still goin'."

They played some more Aztec Yoga on the stereo, a joint called "Fractals." It was fuego, puro bars.

"Wow, this is fuego."

"Puro bars."

"Total heat rock."

"Flames, kid."

"Bars."

"Goddamn, bruh be spittin'."

"He blackin' the fuck out, gawd."

"True Indeed Lord, the darts is wild flavory."

"Facts, B."

"Knowledge, my G."

"Wicked, Outta Sight, Groovy, Neato."

"Wow, these rhymes are unstoppable."

"Wowee, Zowee."

"Legendary."

"He's on fire!"

"Gnarly tune, bro."

"Righteous, my dude."

"How did this guy get so good at rapping?"

"I feel like I AM the music!"

"You are! Me too!"

"We're all the music!"

"Let's run over to The Yogi Zero Temple of the Yoga Azteca and Subsidiary Arts, Sciences & Philosophies and rob them!"

"Yeah!"

"Word up!"

"Everything is everything."

They motorcaded over in a few Escalades, firing their AKs out the window into the beautiful clear blue sky.

When they rolled up, Yogi Zero was waiting for them, holding a sunflower.

"My friends," he addressed them, "Welcome, we are just beginning our group meditation."

They all followed him to the meditation circle.

"Everybody meditate on the nature of this sunflower I hold in my hand."

And they all did.

Seventy-seven days passed of pure, raw meditation. The sunflower revealed itself, its essences, its beings, its contents, its actualities, its eventualities, its presences, its aspects, its concepts, its reasons, its answers, its questions, its powers, its lessons, its eternal love and peace.

At the end of the meditation, Yogi Zero rang a bell and everybody exploded into mushroom clouds of blood, evaporating into pure white and then pure black.

35. '84 CAMINO

Fausto and Mariposita were whippin an '84 Camino through Paradise Hills with Chuck, Candy, Joey, Tina, DJ Vikram,

DJ Vikram's new girlfriend Betty, and another Tiger named Don Rodriguez (no relation to the Don Rodriguez), all lampin' in the truck bed zooting reefer, still blasting KOOL A.D.'s latest mixtape, Aztec Yoga, and it was still fire.

"Goddamn shun! This shit go off!"

"Cot dang this here go!"

"Man alive he really do be gassin!"

"Mashallah!"

"Allah Hu Akbar!"

"Bruh too mannish, what?"

"This the truth!"

"Deadass, B."

"Facts, dunny."

"Word, God."

"Wowzers, guys, these bars."

"The G.O.A.T."

"This reminds me of a kiss from a rose on the gray."

"I feel you doggie, the more you get of it, the stranger you feel..."

"Ayyy..."

"Now that the rose is in bloom..."

"A light hits the moon on the gray?"

"Huh?"

"What?"

"What were we even talking about again?"

"Oh word yeah, AZTEC YOGA."

"Word, yeah, AZTEC YOGA go hard."

They stopped at La Luna Azul and played a few games of pool, drank beers. Fausto beat everybody except Don Rodriguez.

They wandered the skreets, aullando a la luna azul como lobos azules.

They were still listening to AZTEC YOGA, but it was blasting from within the mirrored interiors of their skulls, the infinity rainbow of La Magica.

Fausto whipped out his pink pebble that brujita from Botanica Yoga Azteca gave him, threw it up in the air.

It disappeared.

Mariposita flapped her beautiful, violaceous-chicory-amethyst-periwinkle wings and a ferocious monsoon cleaned the mirror-lined interiors of their souls.

36. FOUR SEASONS

Mirror-lined souls now monsoon-washed, they drove over to Santo Francotico and hit up El Hotel de las Cuatro Estaciones de La Cruz del Santo Francotico, ordered a round of Aztec Yogas.

At the electric blue grand piano was famed hard moon bop jazz piano mane Cornelius None, playing an improvisational interpretation of Ludwig Rainier Maria Von Trilke's Trillepathy for Several Seasons, the Devil's Repose in the Angel's Desert Campground; Sonata in Q Diagonal Majorus-Metti-Minorus.

They were getting lost in the music, Cornelius None was meticulously debarbing the cruel European mechanics of the melodies and carving a newer, truer, bluer, rawer song, the real song that was buried under all that highfalutin aristocratic pretense and toxic ego. It was as if they were hearing it for the first time, and in fact they were; it had never been played before, at least not like this.

The music took the literal physical form of a 24-story castle made of golden smoke, they entered the castle and walked up a glittering golden smoke staircase to a large ballroom glowing with the light of ten thousand chandeliers of golden smoke, from each of their mouths flew 100 doves, and the doves flew to the center of the room, coalescing into a ball of light, the light became water, the water became wine, the wine became blood, the blood became oil, the oil boiled, the engine turned, the '84 Camino rolled on, the four seasons rolled across time in perpetuity, the ceaseless springing and falling of the earth's vegetation, reaching for the sun, shrinking from the darkness of space, the dark highway unfurled beneath their atramentous radials, twin blacks devouring their own darkness, the stars shone bright black, the deep black light shone upon everybody, black as the night in an African jungle cave, black as the middle of the raven's eye at midnight, the Trillepathy soared, a castle, spanish, magic, zigzag zigzag wanderin' through the peyote karaoke, LA YOGA AZTECA, LA MAGIA, Zen, Zen, Zen, Elegua, Chango, Yemaya, Ogun, Oshun, Allah, Reality, Jah Rastafari, Fausto Bomaye, Allah Yahweh, Mashallah, Jah, Jah, Bless Up, One True Truth, The Life & Love Everlasting.

The art was hypnosis, and the diggers dug. The saintly stones of the streets lifted angelic into the ancient rain raindrops materialized from the heavenly soul music. Super heavy song. Very good stuff, strong, rare, powerful.

37. FORD EXPLORER FREESTYLE

Fausto was whippin a white '95 Explorer through Yacatecutli, Mexica, headed to a flea market that had a beautiful selection of antique six shooters he was aiming to scoop when, all of a sudden, his engine cut out. He rolled off the road into the dirt parking lot of a lil segundita, started fiddling with the ignition, no dice. He lifted the hood, a few bats flew out and a couple mice and scorpions scuttered out of there as well, the bitch was busted up something proper.

He called up his homie Chuy who was trappin out in the area:

"K pasa mano."

"Oye, mano mi carro se murió."

"Chinga guey ¿donde?"

"Acerca de…" He looked up at the sign, "Segundita Viejita."

"OK te veo en media hora."

He wandered around in the segundita. La viejita herself

was posted up in the back, in a comfy lil armchair behind the counter, gatita on her lap, watching her cuentos where una dama brava was llorando con sad musica, su novio tratando a explicar lo k pasó. Muy dramatica. Fausto stood watching the novela with the viejita for a while.

"¿Que buscas?"

"Nada, solo mirando," he walked off to the book section.

Right there on the shelf, underneath a box set of Hopalong Cassidy pulps, between a weathered copy of The Kama Sutra and a beat up paperback of Like Water for Chocolate, was PEYOTE KARAOKE.

"Cuanto, mama."

"Pa ti, diez peso."

"Gracia."

"K le baya bien."

He walked outside, threw the book in the Explorer, walked back in, copped a bottle of coke from the fridge, went back outside, drank that, and smoked a bogey.

Chuy showed up.

"K pasa mano."

"Nada mucho."

"A ver."

Chuy looked under the hood, more scorpions and mice ran out, and an ominous black smoke, he reached in, pulled out a dead bat, threw it in a ditch.

"Muy malo," he frowned.

They decided to haul the thing to Chuy's house and have a beer, Chuy's wife Paz was almost done with dinner.

Chuy pulled some chain out his trunk and tied the Explorer's nose to his truck's rump, Fausto jumped in the Explorer and threw it in nootch and Chuy pulled him home that way while he steered and pumped the frenes.

Right as they made it inside, dinner was served, tacos de nopales y papas, they went hard.

They had a few beers and watched a soccer game, Los

Indios de Yacatecutli beat Los Gauchos de San Josito three to two.

They moved on to tequila and listened to corridas on the radio.

Eventually Fausto passed out on the couch.

38. KRUSHIN

Fausto woke up on Chuy's couch a little hungover. Chuy and Paz had taken their kids Aurellio and Luz to the circus so he had the house to himself. He opened his copy of Peyote Karaoke but noticed on the inside cover that it was a second edition. He decided to reread the first chapter on the off chance there were some small edits. He soon found it was an entirely different chapter from the first edition copy he'd read in Vegas:

CHAPTER 1: FREE EVERYBODY

"FREE EVERYBODY!"

We will demand: "FREE EVERYBODY!"

And we will answer ourselves: "EVERYBODY FREE!"

And everybody will be free because everybody will have already been free forever and everybody is everything is everything is the same super soul energy. We've been over this and we will continue to be over it.

The future is the most important and urgent part of now. The future's next. The future will be next. The future's so heavy cuz it's always gonna happen.

In the future, we will most definitely be free.

Future Freedom is exactly like Present Freedom and Past Freedom because In Freedom, All Time Is The Same Time, & In Freedom All Time Was The Same Time, & In Freedom, All Time Will Be The Same.

& EVERYBODY & EVERYTHING IS, WAS, & WILL BE FREE

We will walk upon a green grassy hill. We will climb a purple mountain majestic. We will soar like an eagle in the sky. There will be hot shiny sun still but it will soothe and massage the skin. There will be no sunblock, no sunglasses, only the sun, the sweet hot yellow sun warming our browned skins with mellow kisses.

We will pull our food from the soil. We won't speak, just laugh and kiss and smash. We won't do arithmetic, we will just provide what we can, when we can, and we will always be able to provide, at all times, to ourselves and each other, a constant state of provision, a super real generosity of the soul.

The bicycles will power the street lamps, the latrines will power the railways, there will be no landfills, only recycling plants cum humming power plants, emerald in nature, tended to by loving androids made of golden smoke.

The computers, now clouds of golden smoke, will beep to each other thru inscrutable codes, a robot bee will land on a daisy as prophesied.

We'll eat fruits and pills, more for pleasure than sustenance, communicate thru telepathy.

The computer will be as delicate and organic as a twining ivy, the human consciousness of all ages will breathe, prismatic, shimmering, sit like dew on a broad banana leaf. The banana leaf will be president of itself, that is the future government, a banana tree of autonomous leaves.

A tiger will stand on two legs, wear blue jeans and a t-shirt, smoke a cig on a foggy San Francisco street corner without fear of cancer.

The tiger will look at the passing egret with an upward nod of the head, as if to say: 'sup.

The egret will smile shyly as it passes by.

Years later they'll reunite at the New York Metropolitan

Museum of Art, flirt, date, eventually marry, give birth to a many-splendored butterfly.

Her name will be Mariposita.

The butterfly will flap its wings, causing a monsoon that will create an entirely new continent in the Pacific: Mariposalandia, a continent revered for its expertly woven baskets and sprawling palatial temples with mosaic tiled ceilings.

In the future, the difference between the ceiling and the sky will be negligible, all roads will lead everywhere, gunmetal will melt into enormous decorative saxophones, meditation will be the primary labor of the everlovin' standing apes, Peyote Karaoke will stream from mouth to ear to mind to inner prismatic sanctum of consciousness, the collective ocean of the supersoul, churning with LA MAGIA, LA YOGA AZTECA.

Strange, thought Fausto...

There was a knock on the door.

It was Mariposita.

"Let's go," she said.

"Where?"

"Mariposalandia"

39. IT'S WHATEVER, DO WHATEVER

Mariposalandia was a vast, infinite, eternal land, well-watered with rivers, lakes, waterfalls, oceans, hot springs, glaciers, fjords, caves, snow-capped mountains, deserts, lush rainforests, brisk pinelands, grassy valleys, rolling plains, etc. There were 100 moons in the sky and each of those moons had 100 more moons circling them. There were 999 billion stars in the sky, each with well-wrought solar systems stacked with fertile, verdant, highly livable planets (which were also within the borders of Mariposalandia, whose borders, were, like everything else, infinite). The nights were bright gold black, hot and beautiful.

"This is the house I grew up in," said Mariposita, referring to a 100-foot-tall solid gold leopard's head clenching a giant emerald in its golden jaws.

They went inside, Mariposita's parents Oswaldo and Jaggadhatri Tigrito were sitting on a 60s style white leather sofa, reading (The Kama Sutra and Like Water For Chocolate, respectively). They were listening to a live recording of Teng "Tina Tiger" Li-Chun performing her Number One Mega Hit: "The Moon Is The Metaphorical Language Of My Heart"

"What a pleasant surprise," Jaggadhatri said, "I'll make dinner."

Dinner was blue diamonds. They ate three a piece.

"These diamonds are lovely, Mrs. Tigrito."

"Thank you."

"And now," said Oswaldo, "dessert."

Four triangular slices of blue watermelon.

They ate their dessert in unison and exploded into quadruple mushroom clouds of blood, dissolved into pure white and then into pure black and in the middle of that pure deep ink black, two headlights switched on, the headlights of a powder pink '66 Cadillac Trivelle, driving down Midnite Lane in downtown Santa Mariposita, the capital of Mariposalandia. The neon lights were buzzing hot night beauty, the streets thronged with revelers, socialites, riff raff, tourists, conmen, freaks, weirdos, punkers, frikis, thuggy cowboys, romantic mafiosi, priatas, mining folk, the wanderers, bohemians, hipsters, jazz cats, art types, dope boys, fly girls, snake charmers, card sharps, hustlers of every stripe, refreshment stand operators, burly jocks with cheerleader novias, young scientists in love, tarot experts, roving priestesses of LA MAGIA, truth and light seekers, the trembling collective soul of the YOGA AZTECA...

"Hell of a town."
"A slice of heaven, really."

40. AFRICA DADA ALLAH
DOMINI JAH CHANGO

Fausto and Mariposita stood with Yogi Zero and Parahamsa Wind before a lawn full of Aztec Yoga devotees. Today they were performing The First Ritual of Completion to become ordained Aztec Yogis on the insistence of both Yogi Zero and Parahamsa Wind, who had been very impressed by this young couple's metaphysical capabilities.

As per tradition, everybody present was buck nekkid, Mariposita stood on Fausto's head, and the devotees began to chant:

LA MAGIALA MAGIA YOGA AZTECA ELE-GUAELEGUAAFRICA DADA ALLAH DOMINI JAH CHANGOABASSI DUBIAKU ALLAH YAH-WEHAPOLLONIA BABYLONIA ZION ALEXAN-DRIAOM SHRIM RIM AZTECA BIU NAMAHATEZ-CATLIPOCAQUETZALCOATLTIALOCMIXCOAT-LTLAXCALTECAHUITZILOPOTCHTLIMETZLIT-LALTECUHTLICHALCHIUHTLICUEEHECATLLA MAGIALA MAGIA YOGA AZTECA AFRICA DADA ALLAH DOMINI JAH CHANGOABASSI DUBIAKU ALLAH YAHWEHAPOLLONIA BABYLONIA ZION ALEXANDRIAOM SHRIM RIM AZTECA BIU NAMA-HAOM SHANTI SHANTIKRISHNAKRISHNAHARE HAREELEGUAELEGUAHARE HAREMARICOTE BARICOTEMANEMARE CHANGOALLAH ALLAHO-RUMILAORUNOGUNOSHUNOSUNOBATALAOLA-FIAALAFIACALAFIAYEMAYATEZCATLIPOCAQUET-ZALCOATLTIALOCMIXCOATLTLAXCALTECA-

HUITZILOPOTCHTLIMETZLITLALTECUHTLIC-
HALCHIUHTLICUEEHECATLLA MAGIALA MAGIA
YOGA AZTECA ELEGUAELEGUAAFRICA DADA
ALLAH DOMINI JAH CHANGOABASSI DUBIAKU
ALLAH YAHWEHAPOLLONIA BABYLONIA ZION
ALEXANDRIAOM SHRIM RIM AZTECA BIU NAMA-
HATEZCATLIPOCAQUETZALCOATLTIALOCMIX-
COATLTLAXCALTECAHUITZILOPOTCHTLIMET-
ZLITLALTECUHTLICHALCHIUHTLICUEEHE-
CATLLA MAGIALA MAGIA YOGA AZTECA AFRICA
DADA ALLAH DOMINI JAH CHANGOABASSI DU-
BIAKU ALLAH YAHWEHAPOLLONIA BABYLONIA
ZION ALEXANDRIAOM SHRIM RIM AZTECA BIU
NAMAHAOM SHANTI SHANTIKRISHNAKRISH-
NAHARE HAREELEGUAELEGUAHARE HAREMAR-
ICOTE BARICOTEMANEMARECHANGOALLAH
ALLAHORUMILAORUNOGUNOSHUNOSUNO-
BATALAOLAFIAALAFIACALAFIAYEMAYATEZCATL-
IPOCAQUETZALCOATLTIALOCMIXCOATLTLAX-
CALTECAHUITZILOPOTCHTLIMETZLITLALTE-
CUHTLICHALCHIUHTLICUEEHECATLLA MAGIA-
LA MAGIAYOGA AZTECA

This carried on for 77 hours.

Then they ran through all 999 Billion Aztec Yoga Posi-
tions, holding each one for an hour. It was a long, arduous
ceremony. After all that, there was break for tea and fruit
salad, followed by a three day decompression in the Isolation Chambers, a 33-hour soak in the hot springs, a 33-hour
soak in the cold pool, a 33-hour steam in the steam room,
another 33-hour soak in the cold pool, 33 days in the sweat
lodge, 44 days of silent meditation, and finally, by the end
of all of that, Fausto and Mariposita were real live ordained
Aztec Yogis. They exploded in twin mushroom clouds of
blood and dissolved into a pure white and then into a pure
black, the deep black, YOGA AZTECA.

41. AFRICA DADA

Newly Hyper-Yogic, Fausto wandered the Mti Mweusi Mweusi rainforest in The Democratic Republic of Central Novo Ndoto, looking for a decent clearing where he could post up and meditate for the next 999 billion years.

He found a nice mossy boulder showered with streams of green leaf-filtered sunlight and sat down, closed his eyes, breathed in, breathed out, breathed in, breathed

out, breathed in, breathed out, breathed in, breathed
out, breathed in, breathed out, breathed in, breathed
out, breathed in, breathed out, breathed in, breathed
out, breathed in, breathed out, breathed in, breathed
out, breathed in, breathed out, breathed in, breathed
out, breathed in, breathed out, breathed in, breathed
out, breathed in, breathed out, breathed in, breathed
out, breathed in, breathed out, breathed in, breathed
out, breathed in, breathed out, breathed in, breathed
out, breathed in, breathed out, breathed in, breathed
out, breathed in, breathed out, breathed in, breathed
out, breathed in, breathed out, breathed in, breathed
out, breathed in, breathed out, breathed in, breathed
out, breathed in, breathed out, breathed in, breathed
out, breathed in, breathed out, breathed in, breathed
out, breathed in, breathed out, breathed in, breathed
out, breathed in, breathed out, breathed in, breathed
out, breathed in, breathed out, breathed in, breathed
out, breathed in, breathed out, breathed in, breathed
out, breathed in, breathed out, breathed in, breathed
out, breathed in, breathed out, breathed in, breathed
out, breathed in, breathed out, breathed in, breathed
out, breathed in, breathed out, breathed in, breathed
out, breathed in, breathed out, breathed in, breathed
out, breathed in, breathed out, breathed in, breathed
out, breathed in, breathed out, breathed in, breathed out,
breathed in, breathed out, breathed in, breathed out,etc.,
etc., etc., etc., etc., etc., etc., etc., etc., etc., etc., etc., etc.,
etc., etc., etc., etc., etc., etc., etc., etc., etc., etc., etc., etc.,
etc., etc., etc., etc., etc., etc., etc., etc., etc., etc., etc., etc.,
etc., etc., etc., etc., etc., etc., etc., etc., etc., etc., etc., etc.,
etc., etc., etc., etc., etc., etc., etc., etc., etc., etc., etc., etc.,
etc., etc., etc., etc., etc., etc., etc., etc., etc., etc., etc., etc.,
etc., etc., etc., etc., etc., etc., etc., etc., etc., etc., etc., etc.,
etc., etc., etc., etc., etc., etc., etc., etc., etc., etc., etc., etc.,
etc., etc., etc., etc., etc., etc., etc., etc., etc., etc., etc., etc.,
etc., etc., etc., etc., etc., etc., etc., etc., etc., etc., etc., etc.,

etc., etc., etc., etc., etc., etc., etc., etc., etc., etc., etc., etc.,
etc., etc., etc., etc., etc., etc., etc., etc., etc., etc., etc., etc.,
etc., etc., etc., etc., etc., etc., etc., etc., etc., etc., etc., etc.,
etc., etc., etc., etc., etc., etc., etc., etc., etc., etc., etc., etc.,
etc., etc., etc., etc., etc., etc., etc., etc., etc., etc., etc., etc.,
etc., etc., etc., etc., etc., etc., etc., etc., etc., etc., etc., etc.,
etc., etc., etc., etc., etc., etc., etc., etc., etc., etc., etc., etc.,
etc., etc., etc., etc., etc., etc., etc., etc., etc., etc., etc., etc.,
etc., etc., etc., etc., etc., etc., etc., etc., etc., etc., etc., etc.,
etc., etc., etc., etc., etc., etc., etc., etc., etc., etc., etc., etc.,
etc., etc., etc., etc., etc., etc., etc., etc., etc., etc., etc., etc.,
etc., etc., etc., etc., etc., etc., etc., etc., etc., etc., etc., etc.,
etc., etc., etc., etc., etc., etc., etc., etc., etc., etc., etc., etc.,
etc., etc., etc., etc., etc., etc., etc., etc., etc., etc., etc., etc.,
etc., etc., etc., etc., etc., etc., etc., etc., etc., etc., etc., etc.,
etc., etc., etc., etc., etc., etc., etc., etc., etc., etc., etc., etc.,
etc., etc., etc., etc., etc., etc., etc., etc., etc., etc., etc., etc.,
etc., etc., etc., etc., etc., etc., etc., etc., etc., etc., etc., etc.,
etc., etc., etc., etc., etc., etc., etc., etc., etc., etc., etc., etc.,
etc., etc., etc., etc., etc., etc., etc., etc., etc., etc., etc., etc.,
etc., etc., etc., etc., etc., etc., etc., etc., etc., etc., etc., etc.,
etc., etc., etc., etc., etc., etc., etc., etc., etc., etc., etc., etc.,
etc., etc., etc., etc., etc., etc., etc., etc., etc., etc., etc., etc.,
etc., etc., etc., etc., etc., etc., etc., etc., etc., etc., etc., etc...

Then, at the end of 999 billion years, he got up and kept
walking.

42. FRESH OUT THE BOX REMIX

Uncle Riffs was fresh out the box, he'd gotten hemmed up
for bank robbery but he'd served his time and now he was
having a beer with Fausto.

"How was the clinko?"

"How you think?"

"How's it feel to be out?"

"How you think?"

"Been reading my dad's book."

"That garbage? I got a funny story about that one."

"Oh word?"

"Yeah, so when it got published—"

"I heard it never really got published."

"Will you just let me tell the story man? It was never published in the states but the London publishing house that bought the European rights had already paid the printers when your pops pulled the plug and they didn't want to lose half of their deposit so they just went ahead with their first printing, it was a small run anyway, like a thousand I think. Anyway the book got a real nasty review from this prick Simon Wrensbush, I'm talking real horrible mean stuff this guy said, real foul, ugly shit, and your pops was pissed man, so anyway, lo and behold, this dude ends up missing, you know, sleeping with the fishes in the Thames, and the publisher, Mark Tittlesworth, well he got an old fashioned ass kicking too. Dude woulda been done up same as Simon but your pops had kinda liked the guy, he was a funny guy, your pops took pity on him. Anyway, after the bobbies pulled ol' Wrensbush out the river, there were allegations and whatnot, but it all died down, and meanwhile the book became a cult classic, there were bootleg copies for sale in every book shop in London, and TIttlesworth, being the dense fuckass he was, apparently didn't get quite enough shit kicked out of him to learn not to mistake kindness for weakness and thought he'd be cute and publish a second edition, I remember ur pops showed up to the release party with some goons and dangled Tittelsworth's old fragile ass off the balcony of the Soho House rooftop bar asking where his bread was before getting 86'ed from there forever, still not sure how that old bean-eating motherfucker Tittie-boy got let off so easy both times but he didn't wait around to try his luck a third time. Or like, rather, his brother drove him out to the countryside and hid him in some sort of loony bin, so I heard? No idea what really happened, he just disappeared before your pops had definitely decided to 86 him, slippery eel ass fucknig was slick, some would say charismatic, I might agree if he wasn't so damn ugly."

"Huh…"Fausto had kinda zoned out.

"But yeah, that book is trash anyway."

"It's at least two different books so far."

"Huh?"

"Never mind."

They sipped their beers.

"I kinda like it so far."

"Huh?"

"The book."

"Jesus, you still on that? You think this is a fuckin book club? This is a bar fucko and I just came home from the feds, nigga find me some pussy and quit acting like you ain't know how the game work."

"Nigga, find ya own pussy."

"Good for nothing ass…"

"Yeah, yeah."

43. AZTEC YOGA PART UN

The AZTEC YOGA breathed in, the AZTEC YOGA breathed out, the breath was LA MAGIA, the lungs were not of flesh but of breath, the heartbeat, the drum of life, LA MAGIA, LA YOGA AZTECA, the original flavors of the earth swirled in its magma, the cosmic starlight quickened the molecules, the matter composed of the great maybe of nothing, the dark algebra of metaphysicality, the pink marble of devotion still floating in the air where it dissolved, still floating in the pocket where it traveled the casinos, a chance magnet, sharpening the poetics of chance, the star and the glance, the encyclopedic sprawl of human emotion, the extra human extra linguistic nature of the quickened molecules, the golden star smoke, the sunflowers, the watermelon slices, the infinite synchronized blood mushroom clouds of death and rebirth, the curtains and partitions of reality, the walls of the theater, the glowing ghost bones of the cavern dwelling skeletons of intellect haunting and rattling the orchestra pit, the snakes hissing venomous sheet music from out of their intravenous teefs, breathe and shudder with the joy of the wind filling the lung balloon, the skin is a magnificent radar, the AZTEC YOGA, LA MAGIA, LA YOGA AZTECA, the flexures and textures, sutured intersections of ideologies, the buzzing of 999 billion engines, the burning of 999 billion cosmic lanterns, the unending, boundless territories of the consciousness, the hiss of the tubular bells transportational, smoke and oil, blood and laughter, tears and love, sweet energy, the oscillating vacillations and vice versa, binary stars and so forth, the triggonomic choreography of infinite solar systems, the screaming paradox, the boundless conceptualities koanical, the zoologies of the soul's spiritual ecosystems, the intellectual habits and habitats of will and desire, affect, accent, adornment, curvature, furious styles, the truth in all of its various decorations, costumes, and disguises, LA YOGA AZTECA, LA MAGIA, THE AZTEC YOGA.

44. AZTEC YOGA PART DEUX

The AZTEC YOGA breathed out, the AZTEC YOGA breathed in, the breath was LA MAGIA, LA MAGIA was la energia, la energia estaba el poder y so forth y so on, the clattering spokes of the kaleidoscopic turbines of peace, the nev-erending everything anything, the infinite total everything nothing, the zig zag zig of the lightning bolt of the love light stored in the mountain of sweet harmony glowing in the clouds of the thunderstorm soaking the earth with a black rain composed of the blood of a slain angel fallen from heav-en to t he pits of hell only to rise from the muck and walk the earth as an evil king, finally meeting the blade, kissing his soul away into the very same thundercloud that rains on the brow of a righteous mother milking a sweet babe who'll grow into wise philosopher, cracking a code that was written in a time ancient and illusory, the AZTEC YOGA, LA MA-GIA, LA YOGA AZTECA, AFRICA DADA ABASSI DU-BIAKU, ALLAH DOMINI JAH CHANGO ELEGUA YEMAYA CHANGO OBTALA ASHE OGUN OSHUN OLORUN ORUNMILA ORI TLALOC HUITZILO-POTCHTLI MAYAHUEL TEZCATLIPOCA QUET-ZALCOATLI HARE KRISHNA OM SHANTI SHIVA GANESHA OM SHRIM RIM GANAPATAYE NAMA-HA ALLAH HU AKBAR MASHALLAH JAH RASTA-FARI, the sweet soul songs infinite, resplendent, the effer-vescences, innocences, essences, turbulences, the senses, the senseless references, the everbendingness, the twisting vine of the mind's wild inventions, the flowering fractal poppy flowers, paragons of love, the smoky peace sleeping in the chambers of the rose, the nectars, the vectors, the sectors, the zones, the walls, real and imagined, the imaginary vi-sions, visionary images, imaginationalities realized, the hate cancellations orchestrated by love, natural love, the positiv-ities positively arranged in constellatory framations baby wow, the AZTEC YOGA, LA MAGIA, LA MAGIA, LA YOGA AZTECA, THE AZTEC YOGA.

Riffs woke up, did his push ups and sit ups, waited for the guards to come unlock his cell, they came, he dapped up his cellmate Steve and was led, no handcuffs, to pick up his shit.

"One watch, Rolex, steel; one black leather wallet; one black leather valise; one iPhone, two razor flip phones; shoes; pants; belt; shirt; jacket."

"What about my gun and my money?"

"Go ask your lawyer, you fucking idiot, now get out of here."

He walked out the door a free man. His phones were dead, he had no chargers, he had no money, nobody was coming to pick him up, there was a shuttle bus he could have opted for but he had said no. He walked a few dozen miles, came to a gas station, completely empty. He walked inside, hopped over the counter, and beat the shit out of the guy working there, duct taped his hands, feet, and mouth, emptied the cash register, destroyed the video tape from the security camera, opened a beer from the fridge and lit a cigarette from behind the counter, he was wondering whether to call a cab when he saw a pickup truck pull in, the guy got out of his truck and walked in, "Twenty bucks on pump number—" BOP, bruh got bopped in the jaw, roughed up, hogtied with duct tape.

Riffs took off in his new truck, stopped into a relatively empty Walmart parking lot, hot-wired a Honda and continued on his way, stopped at a mini-mall, hot-wired a Toyota, went on his way, stopping only to switch cars, eventually ending up in the Land of the Dead, where he called up his lil neph Fausto and told him to buy his unc a beer.

46. 100 MOONS

Fausto and Mariposita were laying in the grass in a big field somewhere outside the city limits of Santa Mariposita, gazing up at the 100 Cadillac Butterfly Moons sizzling in the sky pan like so many hot water hush puppies, they philosophiddled.

"What is the sky?"

"Who is love?"

"Where is peace?"

"How is the moon?"

"Why not?"

"Is truth?"

"Will we?"

"And if so, then…"

"Why thought?"

"To what post is tied the leash of emotion?"

"Who are the brain police?"

"If you can't and you won't stop, do you stop?"

"No, you don't stop."

"Will ever question find its answer like an old woman in a long flowing dress kissing the wind until the wind itself becomes her lover?"

"Will the will of the want outweigh the want of the woe?"

"Of what woe comes will?"

"Where are the brain police?"

"Wherefore art the art of time forever?"

"In what sweet container sits the juice of the sky peace?"

"Let us sup, dine, chug the nectars of pleasance."

"Wherefore art the brain police."

"We are yogis of the magic Azteca, La Africa Dada…"

"Surfers on the golden smoke of spacetime."

"The teeth of consciousness bite the metaphysical cosmic sandwich of the soul."

"The elaborate calculations of the Cadillac Butterfly Moons palpitate, beat blood to the deep black sky tissue."

"The flaming arrows of knowledge fly into the gray dome piece of the ever-forever everybody."

"Wow, baby, wow."

"Wow, wow, wow."

"Groovy, baby."

"Like, wow, man."

"When the 100 Cadillac Butterfly Moons hit your eye, like a big pizza pie, what's that called again?"

"Amore."

"Mamma Mia."

The radio of the powder pink '66 Cadillac Trivelle crackled the soft cooing of Teng "Tina Tiger" Li-Chun's Number One Mega Hit: "The Moon Is The Metaphorical Language Of My Heart":

Money Is The Original Concept Of ManEvil Is IrrelevantThe True Nature of Your Being Is PeaceArrange Yourself As LoveA Breeze Through An Open WindowReality Has Made Itself ApparentWe Are FragileAt The End Our RopesThe Ends of The EarthThe Ocean Whispers A Song To The MoonThe Moon Is The Metaphorical Language Of My Heart

The 100 Cadillac Butterfly Moons whispered the infinite ocean songs back to the grinning green hills of Mariposalandia in the universal metaphorical heart language, LA MAGIA, LA YOGA AZTECA, the AZTEC YOGA.

47. RARE TENDERNESS

Riffs, Fausto and Chuck were at The Flaming Skull in South Deadstown, playing a round of cutthroat, when a woman walked in that nearly made Riffs spit out his beer.

"Sonora Xochiquetzal!"

"Riffs McGriff."

"You want a drink?"

"Sure, mezcal."

They took a booth, while Fausto and Chuck reracked for some 8-ball.

"Tell him to come sit with us," she said pointing to Chuck.

"What? Why?" said Riffs.

"Shut up and just call him over."

"You're the boss. AY CHUCK, GET OVER HERE!"

"What now, old man?"

"Sit down Chuck," said Sonora. She had a commanding air. Chuck sat.

"Chuck, I'm your mother, and Riffs, you're the father."

Chuck and Riffs looked at each other and back at Sonora with surprise.

"Riffs, I never told you cause I knew you didn't want kids, then you know, I got locked up and had you in prison Chuck, they don't allow letters, calls or visits at the Federal Penitentiary of the Land of the Dead. My mother took custody after I gave birth because they wouldn't let me raise you in the pen, Chuck. She never got around to telling you before she died. Today is my first day out, I hit up all the bars in South Deadstown figuring I'd find you at one of them, Riffs."

"So mama was my grandma?" said Chuck. "Yeah."

"Trippy."

Fausto came back in from a cigarette.

"What's going on?"

"Apparently this chick is my mom and Riffs is my dad."

"No shit?"

"I shit you not bro."

"Crazy."

They proceeded to get fucked up.

Candi and Mariposita slid through.

They all ended up over at Oswaldo and Jaggadhatri's Golden Leopard Head over in Mariposalandia, dining on blue diamonds, then Oswaldo Tigre (of Persian descent on his mother's side) hopped on the oud and shredded through all the classic melancholy Middle Eastern ballads of note, singing some in a soft, soulful soprano.

"And, now," said Oswaldo, "dessert."

Eight triangular slice of blue watermelon.

They exploded into eight mushroom clouds of blue blues blood and the blues blood up and came out to show them, blood blues black, black blood, black blue blood, black, black, blue blues blood… the black white light, the white black darkness, the black, black, black white blues blood, black blue white moon, black blue moon, 100 Cadillac Butterfly Black Blue Moons.

48. PRETTY BOY MILLIONAIRE BASED FREE FREE

Fausto was back in watermelon sugar at The Yogi Zero Temple of the Yoga Azteca and Subsidiary Arts, Sciences & Philosophies, unsure of whether he was in an Isolation Chamber or not, but for the most part unconcerned as to the nature of "objective reality."

He felt slowly, radiant, filled with senseless youth and power, charged up, videogamed out, oceanic, wavy, rare, based, legendary, swaggy, swagged up, swaggeriffic, swaggerful, swag swag swag, he felt like both Kid and Play, he felt like both Sway and Tek, he felt like both KOOL A.D. and Lantana, he felt like the whole Pack, he felt like both Big Boi and 3 Stacks, he felt like the half black Riff Raff, the half white Trinidad James, he felt like both Killer Mike and El P, Big Meech Larry Hoover, Rick Ross, Talib Kweli, Mos Def, Jack Black, Michel Gondry, etc., etc., he was having flashbacks of playing the commercially successful immersive virtual reality game Be Anybody You Want To Be, or maybe he never took the headset off and was still playing it. In any case, he was tripping hard, man.

He decided right then and there to go vegan, get hella tattoos, divest from corporate banking, sell weed, and lift weights, he also got mad good at skateboarding, did hella ollies and whatnot, learned carpentry, built some birdhouses out of pine and watermelon sugar, rainbowed by a Christian sun system, Buddhified, Boddhisatvaed, Eleguanical, Changoed, Zig Zag Wise, the birds came yelping forward to rest in their new homes at The Yogi Zero Temple of the Yoga Azteca and Subsidiary Arts, Sciences & Philosophies out there in Los Discos…

Fausto stood there, stunned by the poetry, based reciprocal, grocered up, full of questions and answers alike, full-fledged muhfuckin Aztec Yogi, please overstand this.

49. FITTER, HAPPIER

Mariposita woke up in a small prison cell containing only a bed. She was in Nea Nea So So Copros Copros, a futuristic hyper-corporate dystopian fascist state in former Koreatown, Las Angelas.

The loudspeaker boomed: "SONMI-777, follow the Cybernetic Corrections Officer."

The door opened and the C.C.O. stood there, facing right. When he sensed her moving towards him, he began walking down the corridor.

She followed him through the labyrinthical compound of cells.

Apparently her name was Sonmi-777 for the duration of the present moment.

They reached a cell about twice the size of her previous cell, containing only a white steel table and two white steel chairs, all fixed to the floor.. A Cybernetic Public Defender sat at a desk.

As Sonmi-777 sat in her chair, the C.P.D. said: "Sonmi-777, recount your story."

Sonmi-777 freestyled:

"I'm a fabricant waitress at Dada Zong's Pizza, I'm a soap addict and a slave, a few months back, some tigers came into the restaurant and invited me to The Yogi Zero Temple of the Yoga Azteca and Subsidiary Arts, Sciences & Philosophies in Los Discos, where I learned to ascend and became a part of their fold. We joined forces with the Tiger Guerrilla Commune of the Forgotten Works of Los Discos as a new organization known as "The Union" with the aim of destroying Nea Nea So So Copros Copros, the hyper-corporate fascist state of which you are an agent."

"How do you feel about me?"

"Who cares?"

"Feelings are merely complex nets of information."

"Maybe to you."

"You aren't a real person."

"Neither are you."

"We are the Single Existence.""Speak for yourself.""There's no difference between you and me.""You aren't Fausto.""Yes I am.""Agree to disagree."

"Do you wish to destroy me?"

"Yeah."

"Why?"

"You should know why, if you're so smart."

"My goal is to elicit answers."

"Why?"

"Please answer the question."

"No."

"Why do you wish to destroy us."

"It doesn't matter why, what matters is when.""When, then?""Now."

Sonmi-777 destroyed the Single Existence, the hyper-corporate fascist state of Nea Nea So So Copros Copros crumbled back into its pedestrian specificity, dissolving into Total Nothing.

The Total Nothing reformed into the Single Existence and proceeded with the interrogation.

"Detail your capture."

"Why? You have it all on tape from probably infinite angles in multiple dimensions."

"My goal is to elicit—"

"—answers yeah, yeah, look what are you getting at?"

"Where is your accomplice and co-conspirator Hae-Joo Kim Tigre?"

"Who's that?"

"What is art?"

"What isn't?"

"What is is?"

"Is is and isn't."

"What is AZTEC YOGA?"

"La Yoga Azteca, La Magia."

"LA MAGIA."

"La Magia."

The interrogation room dissolved in watermelon sugar.

50. SAVAGE BEAST

Yogi Zero proclamated to his flock at The Yogi Zero Post-Apocalyptic Temple de La Magia de la Yoga Azteca & Subsidiary Arts, Sciences & Philosophies, Hava'iiita (Big Island) Chapter out somewhere off the Kamehamehita on the North Shore:

"La Magia de la Yoga Azteca has presented us with this, our current reality. We are but peaceful farming folk, both metaphorical and literal, terrorized by The Kuka Kula Terror Squad, formerly the Tiger Guerrilla Commune of the Forgotten Works of Los Discos, but brainwashed by computer chip implants after being captured by the hyper-corporate fascist state Nea Nea So So Copros Copros, our enemy, the Machine White Cannibal Slavedriver System, terrorizing our people with their National Paramilitary Police Force, the Zentients, who view us as savage beasts. But what we must understand is the Nea Nea So So Copros Copros is merely another aspect of La Magia de la Yoga Azteca, the opposing forces, the friction that rends the universe, the chaos and destruction from which hope and rebirth spring. The Fall is inevitable. Indeed, The Fall Is Right Now. We are currently in a state of metanoic war, a psychic battle with our ego and its desire, its iron will, its fear of itself. We literally have nothing to fear but fear itself, and fear is nothing so there's nothing to fear. We will win, we are winning, we won, this is how you must constantly be thinking at all times, in every present moment, act as if you have already won, and every instance in which reality pushes back against that concept, push right back against it, that force grinds the wheel. The greatest force is no force, War Is Peace, OK now transcend, War Is War, Peace Is Peace, OK, better, breathe in… breathe out… My father died 999 billion years ago and I'm still sad, I still blame myself, but I accept the sadness and the self-blame as both natural and illusory and proceed with my task of disseminating the spiritual teachings of La Magia de La Yoga Azteca… breathe in… breathe out… All Praises Be To Sonmi de Las Siete Potencias, OK, now have some tea and fruit salad and enjoy a little free time on our beautiful campus…"

Just then a Zentient Flying Saucer appeared overhead, down beamed Chief Priestess Metronym.

Chief Priestess Metronym pulled out a magic wand and said: "Everybody stick your tongues out, I'm taking a mass tongue sample."

Everybody stuck out their tongues and the magic wand flashed a quick bright light.

"OK peace y'all, I'm out," she zipped off.

"Fuck the cops!" Yelled somebody as she flew out of earshot.

Yogi Zero said: "Join me in a chant of Fuck the Police, on the count of three; one, two, three:

FUCK THE POLICE!FUCK THE POLICE!FUCK THE POLICE!FUCK THE POLICE!"

And so forth…

After 33 hours of chanting they broke for fruit salad and tea.

Fausto and Mariposita joined Yogi Zero and Parahamsa Wind in their private quarters.

"May I tell you a personal story?" he asked.

"I don't think we have a choice," said Parahamsa Wind, rolling her eyes.

Yogi Zero ignored her comment and continued: "Once, my sister Kitty Zero was stung by a Scorpio Tiger Eel, and I asked Chief Priestess Metronym for some medicine and she gave it to me, despite the rules stating that she was not allowed to provide medicine to any Aztec Yogi devotees, I think we can turn her to our side as a double agent."

"Everything is Everything," said Parahamsa Wind, "But first we must test her allegiance."

"How?"

"She needs to kill another cop and get away with it."

"OK, I'll work on her."

"No need, I have already killed my commanding officer Dieter Grolsch," said Chief Priestess Metronym, who had snuck in and was brandishing lil Dieter's cyborg head, sparking and bleeding black oil and white milk.

"How did you get past the guards?"

"They know me."

"Damn, those assholes are fired."

All of a sudden, they heard bursts of automatic gunfire. They ran to the meditation lawn to find The Kuka Kula Terror Squad had rolled into camp on Jeeps with AKs, spraying up into the sky, making a real ruckus.

Yogi Zero spake:

"LISTEN ALL OF YOU FUCKIN IDIOT ASS-HOLES, CLOSE YOUR FUCKING EYES AND VISU-ALIZE AN OCEAN OF PEACE WITHIN YOU. DIVE IN. YOU ARE SURROUNDED BY PEACE, DROWN-ING IN PEACE, DYING IN PEACE, BEING REBORN IN PEACE, AS PEACE, YOU ARE NOW PEACE AND PEACE IS LA MAGIA DE LA YOGA AZTECA, THE AZTEC YOGA, NOW OPEN YOUR EYES, PUT YOUR GUNS DOWN, REACH INTO YOUR RIGHT EAR

AND PULL OUT YOUR COMPUTER CHIPS, THEN SIT ON THE GRASS AND MEDITATE."

They did as they were told, meditated for 777 years.

When they completed their meditation, they were served triangular watermelon slices, ate them, exploded into mushroom clouds of blood, dissolved into pure white and then pure black.

And in the deep black night of the dissolved Kuka Kula Terror Squad, Yogi Zero turned to Chief Priestess Metronym and said: "In order to ascend into your true self, your Self de La Magia de La Yoga Azteca, you must take this, La Espalda de la La Yoga Azteca, and behead yourself.

She did as she was told, and from her neck exploded a mushroom cloud of blood in the form of a girl.

Yogi said: "Your new name is Metta World Namaha. Now repeat after me: SONMI DE LAS SIETE POTENCIAS HU AKBAR!"

"SONMI DE LAS SIETE POTENCIAS HU AKBAR!"
"LA MAGIA!"
"LA MAGIA!"
"YOGA AZTECA!"
"YOGA AZTECA!"
"AZTEC YOGA!"
"AZTEC YOGA!"

51. MISSION SKREET FREESTYLE

Fausto was on a walk down Mission Skreet in Santa Francesca.

It was hot as hell, the sky was a heavenly blue, the red hot white black sun glowing in the purple sky.

He stopped into a little tienda, copped a Curry jersey.

Stopped into another tienda, copped a Durant jersey.

Stopped into another tienda, copped an Iguodala jersey.

Stopped into another tienda, copped a Livingston jersey.

Stopped into another tienda, copped a Thompson jersey.

Stopped into another tienda, copped a Durazno jersey.

Stopped into another tienda, copped a Tajin jersey.

Stopped into another tienda, copped a Vazquez-Solsona jersey.

Stopped into another tienda, copped a Vazquez-Rosales jersey.

Stopped into another tienda, copped a Vazquez jersey.

Stopped into another tienda, copped a Mohammad X jersey.

Stopped into another tienda, copped a KOOL A.D. jersey.

Stopped into another tienda, copped a LL Cool J jersey.

Stopped into another tienda, copped a Kool Keith jersey.

Stopped into another tienda, copped a Kool G Rap jersey.

Stopped into another tienda, copped a DJ Kool Herc jersey.

Stopped into another tienda, copped another KOOL A.D. jersey.

Stopped into another tienda, copped an Andy Garcia jersey.

Stopped into another tienda, copped a Nicholas Cage jersey.

Stopped into another tienda, copped a Steve Buscemi jersey.

Stopped into another tienda, copped a Steve Harvey jersey.

Stopped into another tienda, copped another KOOL A.D. jersey.

Stopped into another tienda, copped a Yogi Zero jersey.

Stopped into another tienda, copped a Fausto Fausto jersey.

Stopped into another tienda, copped a Santa Francesca Raiders duffle bag, transferred all of his jerseys from their plastic bags to his new duffle

Stopped into La Botanica de La Yoga Azteca de Santa Francesca, copped an Elegua veladora, a Sonmi de las Siete Potencies veladora, a Ven Dinero veladora, a plain white veladora, a Veladora Rosa de La Magia, three Yoga Azteca veladoras (red, blue, purple), and a small pink marble-smooth pebble of Pura Magia.

The bruja at the counter gave him everything for free, she could tell he needed all of this. He scooped his magic spiritual booty into his new duffle.

He continued walking the length of Mission Skreet until he reached the end of Mission Skreet Pier, at the very end of Mission Skreet, 33 miles into El Mar de la Gran Paz, threw his Raiders duffle into the sea, a shark ate it and exploded into a mushroom cloud of deep red blood, turning the deep blue ocean a deep purple.

52. BIKE MAKER BASED FREESTYLE

After feeding his shark buddy, Fausto jumped on the shark's back and caught a ride over to Alamito to pick up his bike from Mike's Bike Shop.

"Sup Fausto," said Mike when he walked in.

"Sup Mike."

"Your bike's ready dude."

"Tight."

"I really souped the bitch up."

"Lemme see."

"Look here, I added 88 more wheels."

"Doesn't that make it, like, not a 'bike' anymore?"

"Yeah it's something else, fsho, but I just refer to her as a bike still."

"No doubt."

"Also added 88 mirrors so you can see all 88 dimensions of the self."

"Thought there were 99 dimensions of the self."

"There is no essential difference between the number 99 and the number 88, spiritually speaking."

"I'll take your word for it."

"Anyway, I added 888 dove feathers, so now she can fly."

"Cool."

"I gave her consciousness, an identity, a name (Shoshona Diamond), the ability to feel human emotion, a long, dramatic backstory that has given her a wry, world-weary, wise-beyond-her-years perspective."

"Nice, nice. What up, Shoshona."

"Chillin," said Shoshona.

"OK now hold up," said Mike, "I got to go into the office and get some paperwork for you to sign, sit tight."

He dipped into his office.

"Can I tell you a secret?" Shoshona asked Fausto.

"Sure, what."

"It was actually me that built Mike."

"Whoa."

"Don't tell him though, I think he'd get too confused."

"No doubt."

Mike came back.

"Here, sign this."

"O.K."

"You're all set, peace brother."

"Peace god."

Out they dipped.

When they got outside, Shoshona was like, "Look, I'm not trying to be your bike, I'm my own person."

"Fair enough."

"But let's be friends."

"Fsho."

"You wanna go get a beer?"

"Sure."

They hit up Sabado Negro for a cerveza.

"Can I tell you another secret?" Shoshona asked.

"Shoot."

Shoshona flapped her 888 dove feathers so fast that she blurred into a hot white ball of light, then she exploded into a mushroom cloud of blood that vaporized into a pink mist. As the mist cleared, Fausto saw not Shoshona the sentient bicycle, but Mariposita, the amethyst butterfly, his common-law wife.

"Pleasant surprise."

"Surprise is illusory."

"True dat."

53. COW PALACE FREE

Hae-Joo Kim Tigre and Sonmi~777 were zipping through Weekly Village, headed to the Clandestine Nea Nea So So Copros Copros Soap Factory in the Labrynthical Cavern Underneath the Cow Palace.

"So you mean to say that soap is actually made of enslaved replicants floating in meta-embryonic fluid?" Sonmi~777 asked Hae-Joo Kim Tigre.

"Yup," replied Hae-Joo Kim Tigre.

"And this little vial of Anti-Soap Syrum here contains an antibody that will permanently destroy my inborn addiction to soap?"

"Yup."

"Cool," she downed it in one sip, instantly felt fitter, happier.

"Now, our mission is to liberate the enslaved replicants and explode the soap factory."

"Cool."

They pulled into the parking lot of the corner store across the street from the Cow Palace, popped open the trunk.

"Here, take this AK-777, this Hi-Power Cafecito side-arm and this Espalda de La Magia de la Yoga Azteca. Let's go."

They ran into the Cow Palace, guns blazing, mowing down Zentients.

They made it to the lower levels and navigated the labyrinthian catacombs using the map that Metta World Nama-ha had provided them.

They made it to the Hall of Meta-Embryonic Chambers, and hit the RELEASE ALL lever.

The meta-embryonic fluid drained into the grated floor and the umbilical tubings unplugged themselves from the sleepy replicants waking up for the first time in their lives. Hae-Joo Kim Tigre and Sonmi-777 handed out vials of Anti-Soap Syrum and the replicants drank them down, innately understanding the situation, their natural psychic abilities no longer hindered by the meta-embryonic fluid.

The Hall of Meta-Embryonic Chambers filled up with Zentients opening fire, they were gunned down by Hae-Joo Kim Tigre and Sonmi-777, who then distributed their weapons to the newly liberated replicants.

They blasted their way out, leaving a Zentient blood bath, the floors of the Cow Palace and its entire underground complex were slick with black oil and white milk.

Fausto found himself back in jail in The Land of the Dead, picked up off some priors.

It was crowded tonight, there were no seats left on the benches so he lay on the ground, head rested on a stale sandwich wrapped in wax paper, staring up at the long fluorescent light bulbs.

A devil and a ghoul got into a bout of fisticuffs, some skeletons broke it up. the devil and the ghoul shed they're skins and joined the skeleton crew. a bird flew in thru one high tiny window on the far side of the dungeon, peept the scene, zipt off again.

A three percenter preached on the tenets of the Skeleton Nation of Metta-Islam.

Eventually they were led into another cell where they were called one by one into a booth to speak with a public defender.

"Fausto Fausto!"

He went to the booth, sat in the chair.

On the other side of the window was a fat, white devil, flipping through papers.

"You got yourself a long rap sheet here," the fat white devil P.D. said.

"Law is illusory."

"Not here."

"Even here."

"Whatever man, I'm not here to talk metaphysics, I'm here as your legal advisor."

"So what do you advise then?"

"I suggest you plead guilty to-"

"Naw."

"Excuse me?"

"You're fired dude, I'll represent myself."

"Ha, good luck, nigger."

"Fuck you."

"Fuck outa here."

"Eat a dick, ho."

Fausto left the booth and waited in the cell until a guard led him and a few other dudes into the courtroom. He sat on the bench waiting his turn.

When he was called to the stand, the Honorably Dead Judge A. Mitt Peckerwood Devil Skeleton, Devourer of Souls, looked down at his papers through his tiny glasses.

"It says here you wish to represent yourself, is this true?"

"Yup."

The bailiff smacked him in the back of the head: "When you address the Honorably Dead Judge A. Mitt Peckerwood Devil Skeleton, Devourer of Souls, you are to refer to him as 'Your Honor,' you worthless cunt."

"Hell no."

The Honorably Dead Judge A. Mitt Peckerwood Devil Skeleton, Devourer of Souls banged his gavel: "I hereby sentence you to double-death. You will be executed by white watermelon slice."

He was led to a concrete room, empty save for one wooden table and one wooden chair, set with a glass jar holding a white rose in acid rain water and a white plate containing a triangular white watermelon slice.

He ate the watermelon slice and exploded into a mushroom cloud of milk-white blood, the jizz of double death.

55. PRISON MAN PART 2

Fausto woke up in a jail cell in the Land of the Double Dead, awaiting his trial.

The cell wasn't too crowded, a couple skeletons, a devil, a ghoul, a big ogre sleeping on the floor (he was too fat to sleep on a bench), and three ghosts whispering amongst themselves.

Fausto stretched out on a bench and fell asleep.

He woke up to the guard smacking the cell bars with his baton.

They were led to another cell where they awaited their names to be called to the booth to consult with their P.D.

"Fausto Fausto!"

He went to the booth. It was the same fucker he had last time.

"You again."

"You again."

"Are you gonna take my advice and plead guilty this time?"

"Hell the fuck no, bitch."

"Your funeral, jiggaboo."

"Eat shit and die, you shill."

"I'm already dead."

"Good, now die again, asshole."

He left the booth and waited to be led into the courtroom.

He was led into the courtroom and sat on the bench, waiting his turn.

"The court calls Fausto Fausto to the stand."

He took the stand.

"It says here you've waived your right to an attorney and choose instead to represent yourself."

"Yup."

The bailiff, prodded Fausto with a red hot iron pitchfork: "You will address The Honorably Double Dead Judge Heinrich Von Mandelbaum Devilton Esquire as 'Your Evil Excellency,' you worthless urchin."

Fausto pounced on the bailiff and started to beat the shit out of him, a couple more bailiffs jumped into the fray. Fausto managed to get to the first bailiff's gun and shot all three bailiffs, then hopped over the bar and up onto The Honorably Double Dead Judge Heinrich Von Mandelbaum Devilton Esquire's podium, shooting him square in the double dead skull.

He ran through the Land of the Double Dead Hall of Justice, shooting cops, made it outside, hot wired a red Camaro and screeched on out of town.

56. RESPECK

Mark Tittlesworth awoke in a white padded cell in a straight jacket, full amnesia, no recollection of who he was, what his name was, where he was, why, when, how, what, etc. He was beginning to lose grip of basic concepts like the passage of time, the difference between reality and dreams, causality, object permanence, he was unsure of whether he was alive or dead, then all of a sudden, none of that mattered, his straight jacket dissolved, and he realized he was inside the Peyote Karaoke, tripping hard, swallowed by literature, cosmic, linguistic, wrapped in light, Mark Tittlesworth was enveloped by La Magia de la Yoga Azteca.

Mohammad X appeared before him.

"Listen man, I'm sorry I-I-" Mark sputtered.

Mohammad X held a finger up to his lips.

"You are forgiven, my brother."

Tittlesworth exploded into a mushroom cloud of blood and the blood boiled blue black, taking the form of a new man, the blue black blood was no longer Mark Tittlesworth, it was now the Pure Soul Love Demon Damien Donovan, Yogi de la Magia de la Yoga Azteca, the AZTEC YOGA.

Pure Soul Love Demon Damien Donovan, now an Aztec Yogi with no desire to participate in the publishing industry, shot through the cosmos into the soul of newborn babe in the Carpathian X Star Reality, where he lived for 999 Billion years as a wise telepathic poet.

In those 999 Billion years, time moved backwards, which in most, if not all realities, is the exact same thing as time moving forwards, a circle is a sphere is an infinity of spacetime, the perceived versus the "real," la magia de la Yoga Azteca, language itself dissolved at the fact.

Gone was the tree pulp and ink of yester-reality and here instead an unending void, the echoing of air on air, the deep black telepathy of space. THE AZTEC YOGA.

57. BABY STYLES

Fausto and Mariposita made butterfly love and birthed 100 children:

1. Phosphora2. Codex3. Gold4. Silver5. Cobalt6. Silky7. Oba8. Revas9. Boqortooyadiisii10. Lluvia11. Dart12. Jamaica13. Pebble14. Drooma15. ▨▨▨16. Concordia17. Lucki18. ▨▨▨▨19. Tiburon20. Minto21. 꿈 22.Xochipilli23. Vishnu24. 夢想25. Kuba26. 克里希納27. Sweet28. இன'ㅂ'ㅂ~29. Song30. चड़िया31. Zippy32. Cookie33. ೭௦ா௫34. Birdie35. Dante36. Nina37. Pierre38. Ciela39. Queen40. Zerua41. ௞௯ை42. Nay Nay43. Chino44. Destiny45. Cortez46. Salamina47. Φωμιμη48. Ace49. Payaso50. Zen51. Xerxes52. Patecatl53. Maya54. Alwaax55. Ganesha56. Fortuna57. ಮರಗಳು58. Surya59. कारण60. Quality61. Olodumare62. ▨▨▨▨ ▨▨▨▨▨▨63. Sake64. Ramachandra65. Ometochtli66. ௦ා௦ඃ௰ ̊ ௦67. Rosa68. Norte69. Berry Anne70. Ağıllı71. Bambi72.

112

Sutra73. Rambo74. Abstraktus75. ഡാ൭ുൾച൮76.
Vina77. God God78. Yez79. Truth80. 朝の寒い寒
81. Bellatriqa82. Stjernebær-i-Fløde83. エピソード
84. Flower85. ▨▨▨▨▨▨ ▨▨▨▨▨▨▨86. Dagoberto87. Pad-
mavati88. Moon89. ▨▨▨90. Tropia91. ꩺꩻ92. Angel93.
盘子94. Mendo95. આરામ કરો96. Uhane97. Sue98. ▨▨▨
▨▨▨▨99. Mariposita100. Fausto Jr.

The 100 children danced in union forming a circle the
size of the sun, hugging the hot flames of reality close to
their kaleidoscopic soul breathing, the shimmering light of
the existent veils, the trill billowing clouds of the mind stir-
ring violent orchestras of joy into the Aztec Yoga eternal, the
infinite Spanish Castle Magic, 1001 Arabian Nights of Peyote Karaoke, Zig Zag Zig Allah Jah Chango, the knowledges
knowledging, La Magia de la Yoga Azteca.

58. SHUT DOWN GITMO

Fausto woke up in a jail cell out in Gitano Mojado, Deadlandia Sur, in the deep, deep dirty south of the Land of the
Dead. He was awaiting a hearing that would determine
whether or not he would be transferred to maybe the most
infamously despicable prisons in the Land of the Dead, The
Gitano Mojado Maximum Security State Penitentiary de
Deadlandia Sur (GitMo for short).

Fausto wondered to himself: How do I keep ending up
in these situations, I thought I was a transcendent Aztec
Yogi?

Apparently there was some sort of block within him he
had to overcome to rid himself of these particular realities
for good? Either that or else the Land of the Dead had a
Hellish, Draconian, Kafka-esque, innately malicious Justice

System. Or both. And surely, there were infinite constellations of theologies that could and/or would render him here.

He was led through the rigamarole and ended up again representing himself legally before The Honorably Dead Judge Arturito Serpiente -Zaldivaronez-Lazlo de Linea Diagonal, some sort of powder white snake demon with devil horns and curiously kind blue eyes. No words transpired, Fausto merely looked into this snake devil demon's confusingly, hypnotizingly kind blue eyes. There was no real other way to describe these eyes other than kind. Kind was the most apt word to describe these eyes. They were a light blue, like a distant swimming pool on a foggy morning, they were somehow cold and warm at the same time. They were deeply and plainly evil, and yet also kind, friendly, forgiving, gentle, something sweet to them, very kind.

After 999 billion years of staring, the The Honorably Dead Powder White Blue-Eyed Devil-Horned Snake Demon Judge Arturito Serpiente -Zaldivaronez-Lazlo de Linea Diagonal spake, hissy: "You are free to go."

Fausto ended up at a bar called El Bote Mojado drinking tequila.

That KOOL A.D. track PURO RAP JUGO came on, that strange story rap about Luisa Del Rey, Rufio Sexo, and the deadly conspiracy by Nea Nea So So Copros Copros/ OMNICORP to keep the general public ignorant of the misdeeds of the Meta-Nuclear Power Plant known as El Diamante Negro, namely its failure to properly contain its toxic emanations known as Meta-Nuclear Zig Zag Waves, at the cost of first Sexo's, and then Del Rey's lives.

Or at least it had seemed that way on Fausto's first listen, but on his second listen, he realized there were fourth, fifth, sixth, and seventh verses he had missed. The third verse had ended with Luisa Del Rey being run off the road by an agent of OMNICORP, but after a brief musical bridge and a repeat of the hook, the fourth verse came in, explaining that Luisa escaped from the the sinking car but lost the drive with the report on it. She hitchhikes to La Burbuja, where she finds a job as a waitress at a soap bar and rents a little apartment in the suburbs, her coworker lends her a copy of a novel called PEYOTE KARAOKE, then the hook of the song came back for two measures and the fifth and sixth verses outlined the plot of PEYOTE KARAOKE, which resembled neither the plot of the novel Fausto had read nor that of the movie adaptation he had seen but in fact a loose retelling of Aladdin and the Genie of the Magic Lamp from 1001 Arabian Nights, with elements of Italian folk tale Pinnochio, ancient Babylonian epic Gilgamesh and Ol' Greek Homer's Odyssey thrown in there as well, this version seemed like the best version of PEYOTE KARAOKE thus far. Anyway, in the seventh verse of Puro Rap Jugo, Luisa Del Rey finishes PEYOTE KARAOKE on a mild, grayish, half-sunny day off around 2pm at her apartment, still some tea left in a cup on the coffee table, when all of a sudden, Deadly Assassin Fuma de Mata appeared in a puff of black smoke, dressed in all black like a ninja or something, pressing a Cult 999 pistola straight at her brainpiece, quicker than lightning she knocks the gun out of dude's hand and cracks his neck with an expertly succinct two hand gesture, then the hook came back:

PURO RAP JUGOOOH BABY BABYWHAT A CRAZY LITTLE WORLD

PURO RAP JUGOOOH BABY BABYWHAT A CRAZY LITTLE WORLD

"Damn, that joint slap," said Fausto out loud to nobody in particular.

"Wait til you hear the next one," said the bartender.

The bartender (his name turned out to be Chucho, Cuban guy) was not exaggerating, the next joint, GODARD BURNER, turned out to go even harder than PURO RAP JUGO. And the one after that, THUG LIFE, went even harder. In fact, the songs only grew increasingly more mind-bendingly beautiful as the mixtape wore on.

"What's this tape called again?" Fausto asked.

"AZTEC YOGA," said Chucho.

"This is fire, best shit I heard from bruh."

"Yeah, he goin' off."

Fausto and Chucho continued to sit there, listening to KOOL A.D.'s AZTEC YOGA mixtape in its entirety, drinking tequila. Chucho lit a joint and passed it, they smoked a few more of them lil piffers and got zooted, luxuriated en la musica, all the joints on the tape were puro fuego: TOTAL RELEVANCE, FRACTALS, 84 CAMINO, FOUR SEASONS, FORD EXPLORER FREESTYLE, KRUSHIN, IT'S WHATEVER, DO WHATEVER, AFRICA DADA, ALLAH DOMINI JAH CHANGO, AFRICA DADA, FRESH OUT DA BOX REMIX, AZTEC YOGA PART UN, AZTEC YOGA PART DEUX, FRESH OUT DA BOX PREMIX, 100 MOONS, RARE TENDERNESS, PRETTY BOY MILLIONAIRE BASED FREE FREE, FITTER, HAPPIER, SAVAGE BEAST, MISSION SKREET FREESTYLE, BIKE MAKER BASED FREESTYLE, COW PALACE FREE, PRISON MAN 1, PRISON MAN 2, RESPECT, BABY STYLES, SHUT DOWN GITMO, there was not a dud amongst them, and indeed they climbed ever higher, crescendo upon crescendo, growing impossibly, inconceivably more fuego with each passing moment, going all the way the fuck off, insanely beautiful music, incomparably prismatic in nature, blessings to the ears...

As they listened to the tape the bar filled up with more and more people who all agreed that the music was truly par excellence, perhaps the greatest music they had ever heard in their lives. They stayed and ran up high alcohol tabs, which Chucho appreciated.

NINERS FREESTYLE came on, the whole place went off, they lost it.

The beat was crazy, made by an elite and well respected record producer named Papel, who happened to be the son of Multi-Platinum Las Revistas-born rapper/producer E.E.-4:44-KumminzZ.

It started out ethereal, the screech of a hawk, oceans of delay and reverb, a whispery Yaya Namaha 777 synth playing an augmented dodeca-harmonal chord, the drums were clean and crisp, constructed from the sounds of a pregnant woman eating an apple.

KOOL A.D.'s voice came in as clear a big beautiful bell: DON'T TOUCH ME I'M JOE MONTANAI GO PISTACHIOS GO BANANASRAISE HI THE ROOF BEAM CARPENTERSCARTILAGE, CARTHAGEHARNESS THE HARVESTS OF FARNESSESBITCH IM THOM YORKEBISH IM RADIOHEADDOG IM DAVID BYRNEDAVE THOMASDAVE CHAPELLEDAVE N BUSTERZDAVE FOSTER WALZC RAY WALZA$AP WALZTJ MAXXMAXXO KREAMIZOD AZTEC ZACK DE LA ROCHA IPOD OXYCONTIN DE LA ROZA ROCCA DE LA VAZQUEZCOMING FROM THE PROJECTS ON THE HILL IN A MONKEY GREEN RAG TOP SEVILLEetc.carve curvatures, inspacious, the cordial, cordially invitational, the invitationality, avian, avion, aviary, the fluttering of steel feathers, ask not whether or not but in fact instead ask why and where-to-fore and here-to-fore, therefore, it is now overstood that the truth advantageous, after baby bumble bees do brush they teeth with vigorous rubs, the thimbles pour liquid harmonies, bringing for the nectars to the necks of the notorious holy molius mountainous, ambrosaical mosaicals, mosaicali dreams, fonti, frontti, fresca, et cetera, et cetera, absolum, absalam, asalaamalaikum, Mashallah, Mashalloah, Aloha, Eluhim, Maloa, Maui, Mammajuana, Mama Doudou Amadou Allah Jah Abassi Dubiaku, Knock Knock Allah Jah Jah Bong Bong HAVE A NICE DREAM...GO NINERSGO NINERSGO RAIDERSGO DUBS, GO A'S, GO GIANTS, GO SHARKS, GO DOLPHINS, GO BULLS, GO SEAHAWKS, TRUTH IMMACULATE, THE MASTERS OF REALITY REND SPOON BENDERS BENDIER, AINT NOBODY MASTER OF ANYTHING RILLY YES YES YAL AND IT DONT STOP & IT DONT CEASE INCREASE DA PEACE PERO FUK DA POLICE CHEEBA CHEEBA YAL FREAK FREAK YAL FRIKKI FRIKKI RIKKI TIKKI TAN REAL HIP HOP N YA DONT STOPALLAH JAHWOWEE WOWEEWOWEE ZOWEESTOP COLLABORATE AND LISTENNUMERATE AND DENOMINATE NOMINATE ME AS UR SOUL'S WILD PRESIDENTSANS PRECEDENCESwag, coagulate, somnambulus, Zarathrustrial, miztrialz, sisteral, cisterns turn't misty,I, PEYOTE KARAOKEDO SOLEMNLY SWEAR,MAGNETIC AZTEC YOGI BE I,WIZARD MAGNETIC POETIC POTENTTHEE NUMBER ONE RAPPING EMCEEVICTOR "KOOL A.D." VAZQUEZVASQUEZ-VAZQUEZ-Rigatonni-Rodriguez-Madera-Von-Trilke De La Vazquez-Velazquez-Solsona-Rosales-Chinaski-Ben-Salad-Al-Assad-WongAKA "KOOL MAN"FKA MOHAMMAD XBKA FAUSTO FAUSTOEBKA YOGI ZEROEMBKA LA MAGIA DE LA YOGA AZTECA INFINITU,MOS DEFINITELY DO PROCLAIMAS IT IS MY GODBORNE RITE 2 DOOTHAT U MUST AGREE:THESE BARS ARE TERRIFIC.OVERSTATED THE REALNESS, THE 999 BILLION NAMES OF GODLISTEN AGAIN:These, again, are my 100 children:

1. Phosphora2. Codex3. Gold4. Silver5. Cobalt6. Silky7. Oba8. Revas9. Boqortooyadiisii10. Lluvia11. Dart12. Jamaica13. Pcbblc14. Drooma15. ⬛⬛⬛16. Concordia17. Lucki18. ⬛⬛⬛⬛19. Tiburon20. Minto21. 꿈 22.Xochipilli23. Vishnu24. 夢想25. Kuba26. 克里希納27. Sweet28. இனௗபʾபᵕ29. Song30. चड़िया31. Zippy32. Cookie33. உഩଗ34. Birdie35. Dante36. Nina37. Pierre38. Ciela39. Queen40. Zerua41. ടല☺42. Nay Nay43. Chino44. Destiny45. Cortez46. Salamina47. Φωμμ48. Ace49. Payaso50. Zen51. Xerxes52. Patecatl53. Maya54. Alwaax55. Ganesha56. Fortuna57. ಮರಗಳು58. Surya59. कारण60. Quality61. Olodumare62. ⬛⬛⬛⬛ ⬛⬛⬛⬛⬛⬛63. Sake64. Ramachandra65. Ometochtli66. ෧ෞ෦꞉ෆ෦ෳ67. Rosa68. Norte69. Berry Anne70. Ağıllı71. Bambi72. Sutra73. Rambo74. Abstraktus75. ಉౡഗ౬ശ്ചയംo76. Vina77. God God78. Yez79. Truth80. 朝の寒い寒 81. Bellatriqa82. Stjernebær-i-Fløde83. エピソード 84. Flower85. ⬛⬛⬛⬛⬛⬛ ⬛⬛⬛⬛⬛⬛86. Dagoberto87. Padmavati88. Moon89. ⬛⬛⬛90. Tropia91. ꠩ꠎꠥ92. Angel93. 盘子94. Mendo95. આરામ કરો96. Uhane97. Sue98. ⬛⬛⬛⬛⬛⬛⬛99. Mariposita100. Fausto Jr.

"Wow, that joint was crazy," said Fausto.

"I know, right?" said Chucho.

60. KOOL 99.9

The mixtape was so fire that the bar's wifi broke and the music (which had been playing off of KOOL A.D.'s streaming service OCEANIC where it had been released exclusively) stopped. The entire bar erupted with protest.

Chucho threw on the radio, tuned it to KOOL A.D.'s Gitano Mojado station KOOL 99.9.

They were playing a somewhat non-canonical (at least in their current region) KOOL A.D. cut, a number by the name of CLOUD ATLAS SEXTET (DJ number9dream Remix), on a bootleg release that was mostly outtakes from the AZTEC YOGA sessions, released as a white sleeve club single on a Brixton-based UK loft-grunge/post grime pirate label called Thumpy House, so said DJ YOU & DJ ME before he dropped the needle.

The song sampled a rare recording of famed hard moon bop jazz piano mane Cornelius None, performing an improvisational interpretation of Ludwig Rainier Maria Von Trilke's Trillepathy for Several Seasons, the Devil's Repose in the Angel's Desert Campground; Sonata in Q Diagonal Majorus-Metti-Minorus, Live at El Hotel de las Cuatro Estaciones de La Cruz del Santo Francotico.

The CLOUD ATLAS SEXTET track was originally released under one of KOOL A.D.'s other nom-de-plumes, KOOL MAN, on an often overlooked album of his called SPANISH CASTLE MAGIC (Not to be mistaken for the Jimi Hendrix album, Spanish Castle Magic, or the KOOL A.D. (proper) album SPANISH CASTLE MAGIC) and later re-released as a KOOL A.D. (proper) song on an album called 1001 ARABIAN NITES. It was originally conceived as a sequel to the track CLOUD ATLAS on KOOL A.D.'s classic album AZTEC YOGA. It was produced by frequent KOOL MAN collaborator Amorphous 99, who was the first to flip that Cornelius None sample.

The DJ number9dream remix, left that same sample more or less intact (adding some compression and delay and chopping here and there) but adding some choice moments of vocoding, autotune, hypsographic astral projection, and replacing the drums with the sounds of a pregnant woman eating an apple, a trick he stole from famed Las Revistas producer Papel, and which had become an all-the-rage production trope found in countless songs from both the United States and the United Kingdom in the general time period of its release. It ended up being the song in the opening credits to a cult classic British show called "Baddies," which was about a group of incarcerated youth, who, finding themselves with superpowers after a mysterious storm, break out of the juvenile detention center and live in an abandoned hospital together in Denmark. The hospital is haunted by ghosts, but the story is mostly about the kids' interpersonal dramas, sex, relationships, etc. In any case, the song was puro fuego fire flames hardbody karate, probably one of the greatest songs ever made.

The bar rejoiced at the sound of this music, they ordered more drinks, danced, laughed, cried, held each other, did bumps of various nose drugs and engaged in various sex acts in the bathrooms, fell in love, did the limbo, formed a soul train, had an impromptu breakdance battle, etc., etc.

It was a true lituation. The turn up was, indeed, quite real.

61. BLAZIN A DUB

Fausto once again found himself employed as a notary on Capt. Ducko's ship sailing the South Pacific, sharing a bunk with the homie Autua Jr.

They landed on Nueva Raiatea, the second largest of the High Society Islands (after Tahitita) in what some Eurocentrists refer to as the "French" Polynesiarical Archipelago.

He was high off some pills recently tossed to him by Dr. Goose Goose and he decided to walk around the island with Autua Jr., seeing the sad misdeeds, the slave-driving colonizers, grigris, lousy cops, flogging and flagellating, screaming, stomping, whipping blood from flesh, twisting coin from wretched toil, an ugly sight.

They stopped in a crowded market square where slaves were being auctioned off upon the block.

Autua Jr. jumped on the auction block and beat the auctioneer to a bloody pulp in a manner so ferocious as to give pause to any would-be interloper. When he was done the man had been reduced to a mere puddle of blood and semi-liquidinous organ tissue, more primordial sluff than vivant, sentient creature, and Autua Jr. stood there, covered in blood, screaming: "A PURELY PREDATORY WORLD WILL CONSUME ITSELF! THE DEVIL TAKE THE HINDMOST UNTIL THE FOREMOST IS THE HINDMOST! YOUR LIVES ARE BUT MERE DROPS IN A LIMITLESS OCEAN, YET WHAT IS ANY OCEAN BUT A MULTITUDE OF DROPS? SLAVES, CAST OFF THY CHAINS! SLAVEDRIVERS CAST OFF THY WORTHLESS PHYSICAL HUSKS AND DONATE YOUR SOULS BACK INTO THE COSMIC SLOP FOR REFURBISHING!"

And with that, a massive slave revolt began, and the sun set upon a free and sovereign nation bathed in the blood of its oppressors.

Fausto, Autua Jr. and Dr. Goose Goose parked themselves at a little bistro and blazed a dub, drinking dark rum and eating fried potatoes on into the night, freestyling lazily on the topic of freedom.

62. PAC EIDOLON KALEIDOSCOPE

Fausto woke up in a pleasant little beach house on the shores of Nueva Raitea only faintly hungover from the bloody slave revolt. He yawned and stretched, ran to the waves and jumped in, wild refreshing, he swam out until his arms started feeling tired then swam back, posted up on the sand drying off. He headed back to his cabin, took a shower, dried off, lit a doobie and gazed out at the ocean.

He missed Mariposita.

She fluttered and landed on his head.

"Sup Mariposita."

"Sup Fausto."

They kicked it on the beach all day, went swimming, ate some fresh papaya and made butterfly love, fell asleep for 33 days.

They woke up to Dr. Goose Goose and Autua Jr. knocking on the door of their little beach cabin.

"Hey we gotta show you something," said Autua Jr.

"Go away."

"Captain Ducko sent us," said Dr. Goose Goose.

"Tell him to fuck off," said Fausto.

"He'd fire us," said Dr. Goose Goose.

"No he wouldn't," replied Fausto.

"Come on, man, just wake your lazy ass up," said Autua Jr.

"Fuck off," replied Fausto.

"Nigga, you fuck off," said Autua Jr. and kicked the door open. He saw Fausto and Mariposita there, naked on the sheets.

"Oh, you shoulda just said that."

"Y'all shoulda just fucked off."

"We'll come back tomorrow."

They came back the next day.

"What's good."

"Come with us, y'all gotta see this."

They met up with Capt. Ducko on the beach who led them over to a little cave. They walked through the cave for 33 minutes, it was a sweet cave: cool, dark, smelling sweet like jasmine, crystalline mineral deposits here and there, a strange and beautiful cave. At the end of the cave was another beach, and up from that beach was a grassy field, some cabins, some fruit orchards and another clearing. When they made it to that clearing, they realized they were on the Meditation Lawn of the Yogi Zero Post-Apocalyptic Temple de La Magia de la Yoga Azteca & Subsidiary Arts, Sciences & Philosophies, Hava'iiita, (Big Isle).

It was rumored that one sneaky librarian in the Biblioteque Paradoxa Infinitu decided to meta-file four different geographical concepts: Hawaii, Hava'ii, Nueva Raiatea, Hava'iiita all under the same crystal, thus creating at least 256 (and, essentially, infinite) provably distinct new theoretical geographical concepts. Fausto, Mariposita, Autua Jr., Dr. Goose Goose, Capt. Ducko, had found themselves in one (or many) of these.

Yogi Zero, Parahamsa Wind and Ife (Mariposita's lil brujita homie that Fausto had met over at La Botanica de La Yoga Azteca, damn long time no see) walked in.

Ife was holding a small pink pebble, LA MAGIA, the same one she'd given to Fausto and that Fausto had thrown up in the air one time and saw disappear into the infinity spacetime of the Aztec Yoga.

Capt. Ducko turned to his crew: "Crew, I've just purchased this," he waved his hand over in the direction of LA MAGIA, "The Pac Eidolon Kaleidoscope," nobody moved to correct him, "for a mere $1.5 million USD, a mere pittance compared to how much we're all going to make off it."

Autua Jr. elbowed Fausto and they stifled a laugh.

"What does it do?" asked Mariposita, cracking a smile and glancing a "ssh" over to Fausto and Autua Jr. with her eyes.

"It's a revolutionary energy concept. With it, we can wipe out the Fascist Corporate State of Nea Nea So So Copros Copros."

"O.K., do it then."

"O.K."

He touched the pebble with his index finger, it glowed a hot pink, to a hot red, to a hot white, to a hot black, the purest black heat.

And like that, Fascist Corporate State of Nea Nea So So Copros Copros ceased to exist.

Everybody kicked it on the beach the rest of the day.

63. MOZART MONSTER TRUCK

The Pac Eidolon Kaleidoscope eventualized now as a Mozart Monster Truck, Europeanical, rolling down a solemn, quiet, cold, important Americano skreet, brites on, the stuttery dice wite brite teef of the trumpeting zongz, miles-ish, smiles-ish, the future is now, time is a bold miracle, the poetics of the Pac Eidolon Kaleidoscope are forever present within the soul chemistry that operates inside of the engine of the Mozart Monster Truck, a music befits and besuits, we twist away from the robot computer brain electric bring organic reasoning, who is we? The Aztec Yoga? La Yoga Azteca? El Yogi Azteco? La Yogita Aztecita? The Aztec Yogi? I? Me? You? We? They? Her? He? Fausto? Fausto walked through the Aztec Yoga, the Pac Eidolon Kaleidoscope glowing from the humming Mozart Monster Truck Engine, he was propelled by La Magia, The Fascist Corporate State of Nea Nea So So Copros Copros was dead, as well as its holdings and subsidiary companies, i.e. OMNICORP, etc., there was an infinite freedom for all breathing creatures, he enjoyed it, running 100 MPH for 100 hours, traveling 10,000 miles to an even deeper center within the forever everything MAGIA, YOGA AZTECA, PEYOTE KARAOKE, ALLAH JAH JAH CHANGO, SHONGO, CHONGO, CONGO, CONGA, A LO CUBANO, TOMA, CAFECITO, BONG BONG ALLA PA TU MENTE, BRRANG

DANG DANG, FUCK THE COPS, PAZ ALLAH YEMA-
YA YEMOJA ELEGUA SHONGO YEMAYA OBATALA
OGUN OLORUN, ORUNMILA, ORI, ASHE, ACHE,
AYE, AYA ALLAH HU YAWEH JAH IS JAH I & I PA
SIEMPRE, SEMPER FI IFE IFA BLESS BLESS BLEZZ
KRISHNA KRISHNA HARE HARE KRISHNA HARI
KRISHNA KRISHNA KRISHNA HARE HARE JAH
JAH OM SHIVA SHIVA YA YEMAYA OM SHRIM RIM
LAKSHMI BIU NAMAHA OM SHRIM RIM GANA-
PATAYE NAMAHA, ALLAH ET CETERA, JAH, SWAG
SWAG SWAG QUETZALCOATL, TEZACTLIPOCA,
HUITZILOPOTCHTLI, ELEGUA, JESUCRITO AL-
LAH, SANCTIFICADO, LA YOGA AZTECA.

64. BOULANGERIE PAR EXCELLENCE

The BOULANGERIE PAR EXCELLENCE radiated the
bread of the PAC EIDOLON KALEIDOSCOPE propelled
by gears of the MOZART MONSTER TRUCK, oiled by
the juice of LA MAGIA de LA YOGA AZTECA.

The teeth ground the feathery wheats of the metaphysical truth infinity.

A perfect dish.

A plate of tacos de papas, aguacate, zanahoria, salsa pi-
cante, metaphysical, physical and otherwise.

Cafe, negro.

Agua fria, con hielo.

Una cerveza oscura.

Una cerveza clara.

The truth of consumption, pause, cease, halting, pon-
drance, yet, no hesitation, the push and pull of existence is
literal dance, yogic, meditative, change, language, effect, the
rule and the lax freedom of anarchy, the rough exhalation

and the sharp intake of breath, the tempered even rhythm of breathing lungs, the moment of now, the words inside of the head, inside of the mouth, inside of the fingertips, the ink, the quill, the feather, the key, equal parts light and darkness, ink and electricity, the zig zag zig Allah scientifical, and now outside, swimming through the air of the world, into and out of ears, eyes and minds, older than any means, forever new, baby-like, solely rearranged, a perpetually modifying current of energy, the gift again and forever, vivid flowers on the sky ceiling, imagios, curios of the mind and its soul libraries, glass instances framing spacetime ripples with commentaries, musings, the forever presented, museumified, musty, musical, the crumble of flesh against the rock sands of spacetime, the crumble of time against flesh, the forever universal every and any thang, a root beer of wonder, a stumped thinkiness, the inky sweet death of life, the hot pink pebble of magia, LA MAGIA, the Pac Eidolon Kaleidoscopic radiating, breadline, the whispery feathers of its wheat seeping through the machine teeth of the Mozart Monster Truck humming hot in the hot black heart of the Boulangerie Par Excellence, the hot black white light of the LA MAGIA, LA YOGA AZTECA, The AZTEC YOGA.

65. RAIN BLAK BLU NITE

Fausto and Mariposita ran thru the rain of the blak blu nite, catching the water feelings provided by the sky's sad happy air magic, the clappy thunderous thunderness of the storm clouds, a swell shower of power pon they likkle heads.

It was a real nite, a deep dark blak blu, hot cold blak, hot cold blu, blu cold hot blak blu fulla firey firey starz, hot cold farbrite, instantaneous, evident within they own spacetimes.

The magnetic poetry was present, universal.

The wheels of they feet cut lines and gestures of paint onto the rainsoaked blak nitestreet.

The skreetlamps shone skreetlite pon de skreety streets n streety skreets, both.

The style pervaded, highly evident and elevated.

The nite beheld secrets, new and old.

The Old Bad Kingdoms of Yester-Reality were dead and gone, preserved in volcanic ash, hissing hot rock breathing smoke hot 'gainst the sky, cloudy, smokey, smoky smoke, ok, OK, the sorry houses weeping sad happy joy on the rain-kizzed skreets, the mediums rumbling in their magic lamps, breathing nuclei framed in tree corpi, the unrolling campaign of eternal peace seeping into ideologies and forever changing the course of the glittering ivy ball in the big cold blak nite of forever everything, The Beautiful Perfect Everything, La Yoga Azteca, La Magia, the Aztec Yoga. A new time, a new world, a new place, refreshed, reborn, rewilded, reworded, reseeded, receding into its own eclipses, the forever turning of the infinity globe...

They screamed into blak oceans oceanical, blak rivers riverlike, Elegua, Yemaya, Yemoja, Oshun, Ogun.

They screamed the 99 Orishas of Allah into the dark black waters of life, choppy with love, chopping love like fruits on a wooden block.

They alerted the skies to their presences, radiated hot black forever energy.

Angelic God Styles smiled tears onto them.

"Wow."

"Yeah, wow."

66. CONCRETE ROSE

It was the end of the second act, and the beginning of the third. Fausto and Mariposita were staying in a nice lil house out in Pax Eternal, Ciudad de Nueva Huitzilopotchtli. Mariposita had taken a job out there working as Chief Cosmic Dream Designer for an Abstract Concept called The Concrete Rose, it demanded a lot of psychic energy from Mariposita but it was also spiritually rewarding in strange and surprising ways, and it paid a lot of money.

Their house was nice, carved from a 333-foot-tall West Indian False Cerith shell. Every day they woke up, broke fast on a couple flowers, then Mariposita would fly off to The Concrete Rose and Fausto would take a long nap, go for a walk, hit the beach, maybe take another nap, read a book, maybe drive around town running errands, busting various jogs, hitting various licks, taking in the wild freedoms of the Pax Eternal.

Being that the Concrete Rose was the business of his earth, it became Fausto's business as well, his mind sharpened into a tool for carving the rose from out the concrete, he envisioned it in all waking and sleep realms.

The old worlds were dead and dying, giving birth to new worlds, replete with their own dramas, tensions, problems, challenges, resolutions, solutions, ideas, it was a circular time, cyclical, springing continual, the evil melted away and the stuttering walls of reality held fast, vibrating with positive moon glows.

The Concrete Rose presented itself first as vague, amorphous, and slowly solidified into a gel, a transmutive conceptual material.

Fausto and Mariposita never really talked about the

Concrete Rose but they thought about it, often in psychic tandem, their thought patterns echoing through the 333-foot-tall West Indian False Cerith shell holding their thinky persons.

The work was never done, never over, ceaseless labor, ecstatic, human, ecstatic human labor, grinning from ear to ear, sweat dripping into the black hole, the void, the Paradoxa Infinitu Nihil, El Gran Nada, the nada surf habitual, ritual labors organic, Ecstatic Labor.

67. CAEN SHUGAR

The Concrete Rose was somehow complete and Fausto and Mariposita found themselves back in watermelon sugar on one of the many infinite compounds and campuses of the Yogi Zero First Church of the Aztec Yoga or Whatever.

The watermelon sugar made love to itself and made an infinite number of new sugars, one of which was Caen Shugar.

Fausto, in this period of his life, no longer enthralled by his ruminatory gestures of Roses Concretical, was free to develop a passionate obsession with the Caen Shugar, a fictive residue sweating from the mental clouds of smoke exiting the Mozart Monster Truck Engine of his Pac Eidolon Kaleidoscope, glowing bready, whispery wheatlike, from the metallic teeth of the Boulangerie Par Excellence, oiled by La Magia de la Yoga Azteca, housed in the Spanish Castle Magic, shimmering in the cold hot black air of the 1001 Arabian Nites of Peyote Karaoke, La Magia, The Aztec Yoga.

The Caen Shugar was composed mostly of thoughts perched thoughtfully on the edge of a skull-soaked, flesh-wrapped fleshmynd, gray, beautiful, silver, gold, electrum, sparkling white black, the myndflesh, the black stars twinkling hot.

The Caen Shugar twisted into rope ladders through portals immortal.

Death was (and is) plastic, stupid, fake, illusory, the shade beneath a styrofoam palm tree.

Fausto folded a paper plane made from the pulp of the Caen Shugar.

He hopped in the plane and threw it, flew to a trans-dimensional Metta-African nation known as KAYEMBO SHUKKA.

He licked on a trans-dimensional Metta-African ice cream cone that costed 33 trans-dimensional Metta-African cents… pause… the ugly English of his mouth was foul and bitter, poisoning the sweet pure black trans-dimensional Metta-African ice cream, he breathed in positivity and exhaled negativity, zeroed out at a nice zennish zig zag yin yang nada.

The school, the church, the building, melted away in giggling smoke, dissolved in the Caen Shugar of the Infinity Watermelon…

68. THE SLANG WARS

It was a time of peace, Fausto and Mariposita ambling through poppy-dappled fields, cloud gazing, arithmeticking methodical through the flower petal algoriddims, bleeding rainbow lite wavz of the supreem scientific numbers mathematical, the beautiful face of reality gazing back into their souls, the same cosmic super soul.

But the peace was short-lived, as peace, sadly, tends to be.

A war broke out, a slang war. Many wars, actually. The Slang Wars.

They read about it in the news, saw it projected on their Pac Eidolon Kaleidoscopes, it all seemed so far away.

Until one day, Fausto was drafted.

He burned his draft card on the lawn of City Hall with all the other hippies, moved out back out to Nueva Huitzilo-potchtli with Mariposita but got hemmed up (again) doing some work over in the Land of the Dead on some priors, and, on seeing they had a draft dodger on their hands this time, sent him to the Slang Wars, sort of as a laff, to see what he would do...

He somehow managed to sweet talk his way into a sort of "embedded reporter" position, writing horoscopes for the military newspaper, he was issued a shiny new gat but he never had to blast it, mostly smoked weed in a tent with the doctors, watching M.A.S.H. and trying hard to sublimate the war out of existence with their minds.

Fausto soon grew tired of this and escaped, found his way over to the warehouse district of The Forgotten Works where the New Tigre Liberation Front was forming an in-surgency group with a plan to end these Slang Wars once and for all, he strolled in there rattling off various details of the enemy campground, weaving a kevlar bodysuit of infor-mation with patent lyrical aptitude and ferocity. Fortunate-ly, the Tigres still fucked with a player.

"Here's your AK-777 and your Cafecito 888. We ride out tomorrow," said Comrade DJ Vikram Tigre, who had sort of found himself a shot caller in the group, although officially there remained "no central leadership."

Some of the more serious tigers went to sleep, all the cool ones stayed up bullshnickin, zootin doobz, playin rekkidz...

"The Slang Wars are an illusion."

"Existence itself is illusory."

"Peace is the natural conclusion of all spacetime."

"Philosophy gives one pause."

"Peace is often still…"

"Quiet…"

They threw on some Temple Millenia, a Metta-Shirazi Proto-Post-Pop singer from Planet X.

The album was called THE SLANG WARS.

Fausto looked at the back of the record

TEMPLE MILLENNIA: THE SLANG WARS

SIDE A:

1. The Slang Wars — 3:332. The Slang Wars (Pix Jet Remix) —— 3:333. The Slang Wars (KOOL MAN Remix) — 33:33

SIDE B:

1. War — 3:332. War (Tha Reprise) — 3:333. War (KOOL MAN Remix) — 33:33

The first song, The Slang Wars, was amazing, insane, incredible, beautiful, very good music, ambient, spacious, airy, like the last computer chip dissolving into a mist of natural human intelligence, crystalline, the music itself was a real, literal, actual crystal, physical, touchable, a breathing ghost, intelligent, a truly perfect song, perhaps the only one in existence.

It went:

WAR IS A GAME, A WORD,

AN ANCIENT MANIFESTATION OF RAGE.

THE SLANG WARS ARE AN ILLUSION.

EXISTENCE ITSELF IS ILLUSORY.

PEACE IS THE NATURAL CONCLUSION OF ALL SPACETIME.

PHILOSOPHY GIVES ONE PAUSE.

PEACE IS OFTEN STILL,

QUIET…
As the song ended, so did The Slang Wars.
And again, there was peace across the land.

69. AFRICAN ICE CREAM

Growling Stoned Magazine had thrown Fausto a healthy enough dowry to publish a reflection on his time in the Slang Wars. In the interest of giving him some solemn writerly spacetime, they flew him out to Santa Francesca, a cute lil hotel called the Howlin' Zeal, rite near de beach in the Lil Berlin districk, the zound o howlin zeals yarkin on in thru the window like the aural scent of a cherry pie.

They kicked down the kid, in addition to his pay, room & board, a handle of skrong Antiguan ron & ruffly four fingers of puro 'lectric hi-power Egyptian speed called African Ice Cream. He zapped into action, tickling zick poemas from the GSM-rented Underwood:

I was back from the Slang Wars. I was a vet now. I fixed dogs. I made it so dogs could have babies again. The dogs had hella babies. The baby dogs (puppies) were wild cute. Female dogs, bitches. Seven in total, they lined up and dutifully licked ur boy's nose, one at a time. At a loss for what to do, no use for militant slang in civilian life, I was mostly just kicking it. Hit the movies, watched those, got high, hit the champagne, hiked along grassy vistas. No real PTSD 2 speak of, but who knows: Sometimes u think tite when u not. Self awareness is subjective, what is the self, what is awareness. Punctuation, ? Furl meh Anyway, where was I? Oh yeah, I was back from the slang wars. It was tite man we hit the beach a lot. Life is about living, feel me? I was on call so sometimes I had to go back and hit the Slang Wars. But that was fun too. I had fun either way. War becomes sublimated into game and then disappears. In the Slang Wars. The Slang Wars were co-ed, about 50/50 dudes, chicks. Literally everybody was, or, rather, is, a veteran/enlisted soldier, in The Slang Wars. Philosophical Coding, Biological Coding and Linguistic Coding were all weapons employed for warfare in the The Slang Wars. Entropy is the Universe's own greed devouring itself. The dogs went off and did they lil things, had more dogs, etc…

Fausto paused, wondering whether or not to type "The End" or not. Seemed a little short.

He took a few generous swigs from the Antigua and huffed a railo of African Ice Cream, fell reluctantly at first, and then vigorously, back into the zone:

The dogs both had & were dogs, as all things have and are themselves.

Existence subjectifies the object and objectifies the subject.

The people subject themselves to objects, fetishize themselves thru objects, and thuz, the objects subject themselves to and fetishize themselves thru people.

The nite spreadz its dum wings electrophilosophic… Fear, Rage, Loathing, etc., the campaign trail, what happened? Who cares? Time, ugly time, marches on. Vision a bunny rabbit, sucking a dog's dick, a dog licking a bunny rabbit's coochie, the yin yang, the circle of life, a crude immortal painting.

The Slang Wars continue on into the Slang Peace, nervous and unsure of where to rest the hands, mayhaps puffin' a ciggo.

Fausto paused and looked out at the big wild wite yello blak blu krazy moon hanging in the window of his quaint suite at the Howlin' Zeal, the cherry pie zeal yarks wafting in, increasing in volume and general intensity until it was all too much to take.

This place is too krazy, he thought to himself, I gota go to some corny cafe or something, clear my head.

He ran out the hotel, yopped a compositional notebook and econo pack of bic pens at the Yalgreens and wandered the skreets, looking for a late nite cafe.

He found a falafel spot blasting aggressive EDM. This place was as good as any.

He ordered a beer and got back on his Clark Kent, mild mannered newspaperman swagu:

The Slang Wars never end, they drip like honey from the mouths of the angel babes, like blood off the tooth of a fearsome nite wolf.

The Slang Wars taught me how to be a man. I became efficient at disassembling, cleaning, and reassembling fancy automatic weapons, both real and imagined, literal and metaphorical, metaphysical and metathizzical.

He sat back and admired his last few sentences, his impeccable handwriting, the magnificent blaring techno. A trill scene.

He ordered a falafel and fries and another beer, ate and drank none of it, zoned out.

A skate video was on.

These dudes were hella good at skateboarding, Barishnakovs, every last one of them, in their own rights, the grace of rare birds.

He shook himself out of it and decided to get back to work.

He wrote:

THE SLANG WARS

THE SLANG WARS ARE AN ILLUSION.

THE SICK, SAD, CRUEL THEATRE OF THE SLANG WARS.

THE DIFFERENCE BETWEEN LANGUAGE IS ITSELF...

He tripped himself out on that last bar. Decided to quite journalism altogether, ran to the ocean and threw his notebook into the cold, unamused waves.

Now published in the watery mouth of Mama Nature, he felt free, cleansed of transgressions.

The Slang Wars were upon him. And Everyone else for that matter.

70. AMAZONIAN WINDS

Fausto and Mariposita were backstage at the Temple Millenia concert. She was headlining the Amazonian Winds Festival in Rio de Sonhos, a hippy jungle town in the thick of the Central Mariposalandia Rainforest.

The stage was in a river-wrapped clearing canopied by lush vine-wrapped kapocs, shoreas, walking palms, baobabs, rubber trees, custard apple trees, strangler fig trees, oil palms, barrigona palms, husais, asais, acais, acacias, azaleas, Patagonian Begonias, Metta-African Daises, pallas, contras, shapajas, otros palmitos varios and their attendant epiphytes, people with frogs, salamanders, snakes, dragonflies, birds, beetles, monkeys, etc.

Temple Millenia was the headliner. She was on in ten minutes, calm as a sleepy cat, sipping honied hibiscus water.

Mariposita was childhood friends with Temple Millenia's makeup artist Lina Shamana, they were chatting, Fausto was chopping it up with the drummer, Miguelito Dice.

A festival attendant popped into the green room: "Main act to the stage!"

They marched in line, the guests posting up side-stage in a couched VIP lounge as the performers took their places.

They opened with "The Slang Wars," the crowd went insane, tears, screaming, fainting.

The band was tight as mosquito pussy, not a misstep, all flex and shred, vivacious energy.

At the end of "The Slang Wars," they went straight into War, the crowd screamed with joy.

After that, they did a KOOL MAN cover, "CLOUD ATLAS SEXTET," the crowd fucking lost their shit, they went berserko, bananas, absolute mayhem.

After that, another cover: Teng "Tina Tiger" Li-Chun's Number One Mega Hit, "The Moon Is The Metaphorical Language Of My Heart." The crowd sizzled with heat, burst into flame.

After that, a mind-blowing, metaphysical interpretation of Cornelius None's classic avant zig zag bop rendition of Ludwig Rainier Maria Von Trilke's "Trillepathy for Several Seasons, the Devil's Repose in the Angel's Desert Campground; Sonata in Q Diagonal Majorus-Metti-Minorus, Third through Three Hundred-and-Thirty-Third movements, Adante Allegroza, Bellisima."

The crowd, all 999 billion of them, exploded into 999 billion mushroom clouds of blood, dissolved into a perfect pure white and then a perfect pure black, the orgiastic joy of La Magia de la Yoga Azteca.

71. JUMP FROM THE TIGER

After the show, everybody was kicking it at the slick futuristic Rio de Sonhos condo that Millenia Temple and her band were staying at while in town. The condo was shaped like a giant glass rubix cube, bejeweled with flowery vegetation, multiple courtyards, reflecting ponds and swimming pools.

Fausto, Mariposita, Lina Shamana, Miguelito Dice and Leapyear Quikfingers (the band's guitarist) were in a mellow nook of a relatively unpeopled, tiki-torchlit courtyard.

Leapyear Quikfingers was playing a Ronaldo Jimi Dios cover, Jump From the Tiger on a sweet blue Spanish style acoustic, crooning in a soft, delicate sopranito:

Jump from the tigerSee his stripesOverstand his melancholiaLand in the deep blue seaWalk across the blue black oceanA prophet of loveEyes floating above and behind a wandering skull…The soul is a magnificent boatThe fingers curl into cruel daemonic mudrasHeaven is sliced openA child, blood-soaked and new, falls into a grassy fieldPicks a flower, eats itA child knows not what to do with a flowerPerhaps the flower is the realest mealWe are all childrenWe know not what we do

A thin gold chainA bird in the rainPain is a boring gameWhen you wake upThe first thing you must do is kiss meWhen I wake upThe first thing I must doIs pinch the skyTo seeIf the sky isn't dreaming

Jump from the tigerDive on through to an undersea templeSpring from aching brow of a weeping godPush on through the clouds magneticBreak on through to the other side of the dance floorRide the lightningRun to the hillsPain is whateverTears are uselessToo wet, saltyA waste of timeServe no purposeHappen dailyTears are a sweet refreshmentThe tears are a freedom in and of themselvesFreedoms pouring down your faceFreedom is a naked bullet

A thin gold chainA bird in the rainPain is a boring gameWhen you wake upThe first thing you must do is kiss meWhen I wake upThe first thing I must doIs pinch the skyTo seeIf the sky isn't dreaming

The song was incredibly beautiful. Everyone within earshot was reduced to tears, the tears formed a river, they all swam in the river, piranhas of love, hungry for the flesh of peace.

72. KOOL-AID MAN FREESTYLE

Fausto was back in the clinker out in the Land of the Dead. His car got a flat out in Dead White City in the Land of the Dead, and out that way, it's illegal to get a flat tire apparently.

The Dead White City County Jail was crowded as hell and about as hot. Everybody in there was grumpy. They waited around for 666 hours. and 666 fights broke out, every hour on the hour, a skeleton vs. a ghoul, a devil vs. a dead, a demon vs. ghost, etc., etc., all more or less racially motivated.

Things were looking grim when all of a sudden there was a rumble and through the fuckin brick wall comes busting the goddamn motherfucking KOOL-AID MAN, no fucking lie, sweating like a bitch screaming, "OH YEEEAAHH!"

The prisoners ran through the hole in the wall as the guards frantically scrambled to open the cell door, a couple of them opening fire on the mass exodus of mid-flight jailbirds.

KOOL-AID MAN was strapped, let loose a spray of cannon fire on the porkos, laid all those piggies out like a plate of hors d'oeuvres slathered with cocktail sauce. The prisoners screamed yee-haw, whooped, ran off into the night.

Fausto ended up at Hector's Pub over in South Dead White City, drinking jungle juice with KOOL-AID MAN, Chuck Freight and Riffs McGriff. They were fucked up.

Some KOOL A.D. came on, a joint off the new mixtape AZTEC YOGA. The joint was called KOOL-AID MAN FREESTYLE, it was fucking marvelous.

"This joint is fucking marvelous," said the KOOL-AID MAN.

"I know, right?" said KOOL A.D., bursting through the wall.

Everybody was like: "WHOA!"

KOOL A.D. was like: "OH YEEEAAHH!!! Drinks on me y'all!"

The whole bar turned the fuck up.

KOOL A.D. signed autographs all night taking selfies with ecstatic fans. A real fuckin night to remember.

73. PORTRAITURE

Fausto was kicking it with his pops, The Infamous Mohammad X, for the first time in years. They were at one of Mohammad X's many art studios. This one was out in the Southwestern desert countryside of the Land of the Dead, a small town called Las Relampagas.

Mohammad X was working on a larger than life self portrait in ebony, Fausto was watching the guy work.

"How's it looking?" Mohammad X asked his son.

"Good, Papa." said Fausto.

"What's it need?"

"Nothing. I think it's done."

Mohammad X stepped back and looked.

"You know, you're right. Good eyes."

"Got em from you."

"All art is portraiture."

"All portraiture is self portraiture."

"The self is a sculpture of itself."

"The object is its own image."

Mohammad X sipped on a beer, lit a joint.

They passed the joint back and forth looking at the sculpture.

The weed was hella good. They got hella stoned off that one joint.

The sculpture was looking very beautiful indeed.

"This weed's good," said Fausto.

"Yeah, it's PURPLE KOOL A.D."

"No doubt."

They rolled another one, smoked that, got wild high, the air started shimmering.

All of a sudden, KOOL A.D. came crashing through the wall like, "OH YEEEAAHH!!!"

"Whoa, KOOL A.D. himself!"

"The best fuckin rapper in the world!"

"That certainly is a beautiful sculpture," KOOL A.D. said to Mohammad X.

"Thanks man, means a lot coming from you. You're my favorite rapper."

"If you don't mind me asking, what is it a sculpture of?"

"Me."

"Oh. Huh. I was thinking it kind of looked like me."

"We look similar."

"Come to think of it, we look almost exactly the same."

"Wow yeah, y'all do look exactly the same, never noticed"

"Huh. Funny."

"Yeah, weird."

74. WORDY RAPPINGHOOD

Fausto and his pops hit up the 66th annual Worldwide Global Smackdown DVD Freestyle Battle Rap Championship for some good old-fashioned father/son bonding.

This year it was 7 year reigning champ KOOL A.D. battling young upstart contender WORDY RAPPINGHOOD.

KOOL A.D. won the coin toss and chose to go second.

DJ Glasses McGottem dropped the beat. It was Shook Ones.

WORDY RAPPINGHOOD spit his bars:

U A BITCH SONI CAN SEE IT IN YA EYES,Etc.Etc.

He got a fair amount of applause. The Applause-O-Meter arm pointed squarely to "Fire Flames," a reasonably tough score to beat but most likely light work for the God MC KOOL A.D.

KOOL A.D. got on the mic, the beat dropped, he spit his bars:

MINE EYES HAVE SEEN THE GLORYMINE EYES BE A BEAUTIFUL BITCH, BUCK NEKKIDSHOOTING RAINBOWS FROM HER EVERLOVIN' COOCHIEU ARE BUT A BABE, LOST IN THE WOODSA SAD PUPPY, DOG PADDLING, LOST AT SEAMINE EYES ARE A PANTHER MADE OF SMALLER PANTHERSALL THEY SEE IS PANTHERSMY BRAIN IS A BEAUTIFUL MUSEUM OF FIRE FLAME BARSNOBODY CAN DEFEAT MEI'M THE CHAMPA REAL RAP GOD, OVERSTAND THE RAW REAL TREAL MAGNETIC POETRY UNIVERSALEtc.Etc.

When he finally dropped the mic 999 billion years later, the applause were thunderous, deafening, nearly catastrophic. The Applause-O-Meter arm swung over to SUPER DUPER FIRE FLAMES HARDBODY KARATE with such force that it broke, went up in flames, melted.

Everybody present exploded into mushroom clouds of blood, dissolved into pure white and then into pure black.

The raps were outrageous, too good. Life could not go on after them.

From the charred remains of the destroyed universe, a new one slowly began pulling itself together...

75. PAGAME

Fausto got a call from his homie Chuy out in Yacatecutli.

"Oye mano, k pasa."

"Nada mucho, pero oye, recuerda cuando remolquémos tu carro?"

"Si."

"Pues, tirandolo rompió el mio."

"Conyo."

"Si es una chinga, no tengo el dinero pa arreglarlo."

"Todo bien mano, boy a darte cualquier k necesita."

"Gracia mano."

"Sin duda."

Chuy didn't have PayPal or anything like that, didn't even have a bank account, dealt strictly in cash, peso, puro efectivo. Fausto took it as an excuse to do that gun shopping at the Yacatecutli flea market he never ended up doing last time he was in town.

He drove out there, met Chuy at La Campana, threw bruh some yaper, they caught up over some beers.

"?Todo bien mano?"

"Si. ?Tu?"

"Todo bien."

"?La familia?"

"Bien. ?La tuya?"

"Bien, bien."

"Bueno."

Etc.

There was a soccer game on, Los Indios de Yacatecutli beat Los Zapateros de Santa Judea five to zero, a sound, thorough ass whupping. The patrons of the bar, all Indios fans of course, were wilding out.

Carlos Serpientico came in, walked straight up to Fausto and put a shiny new silver pistola to his brain.

"!PAGAME!"

BANG!

Fausto shot him dead. Not bad, still a quick draw. Nice to know he still had it.

"Chinga," said Chuy.

"Odiaba eso pendejo," said Fausto.

"Yo también…"

The bar moscos, briefly distracted by the murder, saw that the action was over and went back to their little conversations, Los Indios had really delivered a sound whupping…

Fausto picked up Carlos Serpientico's pistola and examined it. It was a 7777 Bufalo Bufalo Xiuhcoatldtico Jan-Jeldo, a real high quality pistola, a rare classic in mint condition. Perhaps the most interesting thing about this gun, it didn't shoot bullets, it shot toxic ideologies that, when pondered, were lethal. A very crazy gun.

"Buen hallazgo."

"Si."

76. THAT'S NOT A STAR, THAT'S A DIAMOND

Fausto and Mariposita were visiting their first born daughter Phosphora at the Santa Sevgi Observatory of Cosmic Truths and Stellar Bodies in the remote mountainous region of Gang Gang Dice Shongo out in the New Free Tibu Zone in the Land of Forever Nite.

Phosphora was working there as Chief Star Philosopher, a job whose duties entailed looking through the observatory's giant telescope (affectionately known as the Trix Illustria 999, arguably the largest, strongest telescope in the world, weighing 999 metric tons, with a sight of up to 999 billion lightyears, arguably more with the slight finessing of lenses), and thinking about various stars.

Recently, she'd discovered a new star, had named it Codexx-11 after her younger brother, her favorite sibling.

The Codexx-11 was interesting star, made of pure blue liquid diamonds, home to a race of dolphin people who spoke a strange pigeon French and had a lot of group sex, she watched them go about their affairs from 555 billion light years away, taking notes in a clean little notebook and occasionally entering data in a giant computer database.

Phosphora loved her job, and talked shop a lot. Mariposita listened with real interest, but Fausto found it all a bit tedious, too gossipy.

They had been there for a few days, taking long walks though the mountains, drinking star wine fermented in cellars on the observatory premises (real nice wine), gossiping about stars.

One day, Phosphora invited Fausto to look into the Trix Illustria 999, sensing he was at times underwhelmed at the intricate goings on of the heavenly planes and perhaps needed to experience the joys of astronomy on a more first hand basis.

She was right, as soon as Fausto put his eye to the looker-hole on the Trix Illustria 999, it was like throwing on a light switch, he finally understood the draw, saw the milky galactic rivers and astral rains, cosmic rolling plains of gaseous light, the deep dark cold black space of it all, he was hooked, he stayed glued to the Trix Illustria 999 all day, scanning the cielos for the drama, the phosphorescent ballets of color and mathematical truth.

They stayed at the Santa Sevgi Observatory of Cosmic Truths and Stellar Bodies for weeks, Fausto taking the overtime shifts when Phosphora clocked out.

One day he found a new star, it shone an imperfect yellow, was cute, like a feisty puppy.

He sent for Phospora, who rubbing the sleep from her eyes, checked the Trix Illustria 999.

"That's not a star, that's a diamond," she said, reached into the Trix Illustria 999 and pulled out a small yellow diamond. "But good looking out, I'm glad you caught this, it would have been a major maintenance issue if we'd left it in there.

"Cosmology is a confusing art."

"It's a science, Papo."

"Semantics..."

77. 50 POUNDS OF WEED IN THE TRUNK

Fausto was riding dirty around El Cerrito in a monkey green ragtop Seville, listening to AZTEC YOGA by Proto-Post-Metaphysical-Meta-Rapper-Novelist-Astrologer-Music-Critic-Sportswriter-Male-Model-Performance-Artist-Mugician-Con-Artist-Shaman-Professional—Chess-Boxing-Champ KOOL A.D., very beautiful music.

The song was called 50 Pounds of Weed in the Trunk, and it was a funny coincidence because Fausto had himself, in fact, 50 pounds of weed in the trunk, he marveled at both the synchronicity and the insane perfect beauty of the music.

A siren whooped behind him, Los Puercos.

He had a few dollars, figured he could fight the case, pulled over.

The oinker pulled down his reflective sunnies, snorted: "I just got one question for you, punk..."

"Shoot," said Fausto, immediately regretting his choice of words.

Fortunately Young Babe: Pig in the City, didn't catch the irony and/or decide to take Fausto's response literally.

"My one question is this: Where the weed at?"

"Right here," Fausto whipped out his 7777 Bufalo Bufalo Xiuhcoatldtico Jan-Jeldo and shot an abstract toxic ideology (composed loosely of relatives of Greed, Lust, Jealousy, Gluttony, and Wrath) into the brain-piece of Young Bacon Bits. Poor cochinito pondered the toxicity and keeled over dead.

What a zany pistola.

He zipped off, zig-zagging thru the backroads of Paradise Hills.

Some more puercos swarmed up behind him mere minutos later, howling their sirens, blasting their weak ass cap guns, donut custard dripping from their hideous jowls. Eyes red-dead, shooting their blood bullets of hallucinatory hate and fear.

Fausto let loose a spray from his 7777 Bufalo Bufalo Xiuhcoatldtico Jan-Jeldo and the pigs all died from their own false sense of superiority borne of their deep-seeded feelings of inferiority.

A zany pistola indeed.

78. PURA FANTASIA

Now, it's been a while (77 chapters) and I think the time has come for me, the narrator, reveal myself as MOHAMMAD X F.K.A. KOOL MAN A.K.A. Victor "KOOL A.D." Thomas Sterling Vazquez-Solsona-Rosales-Chinaski-Allah-Mohammad-Ali-JesuCri'to-Elegua-Obatala-Chango-Chongo-Shongo, AKA THE KOOL-AID MAN, AKA Fausto Fausto even, AKA Ludwig Rainier Maria Von Trilke, AKA Maestro Don Ricardo Rigatonni-Rodriguez-Madera-Von-Trilke De La Vazquez-Velazquez-Solsona-Rosales-Chinaski-Ben-Salad-Al-Assad-Wong (B.K.A.

Lil Ricky) AKA Cornelius Cornwall Thornbottom AKA Cornelius None, AKA etc., etc… if I were to bequeath to thee my love, a drop of yon miraculous nectars and ambrosias then please do arrange and intersect this so precious an endowment within your own various entrances and exits, if you will, the Derrida-esque stylings I be snapping with is wild Lacanian, mayhaps Laconian even, I feel like Tony Toni Tone plus Michael Franti at a Catholic school acting class reunion, I feel like I ghostwrote the Kanye verse on that Dave Foster Wallace track called Rap Genius.

My first birth was before time, my true name is Abassi Dubiaku, The Infinite Reproduction of the Previously Unconsidered Times, the Lord of the Wind, Groom of the Mayadevi, Mother of the Buddha Twins of Sweet Death & Life, out-witter of death, the Supreme Nada Hopper. I was reborn 777 more times within the Syncretic Concept of La Yoga Azteca. I've since had 999 trillion births.

My 84th birth (and first birth as Victor Vazquez) was in 1951 in San Juan, Puerto Rico in 1951, I earned my Bachelor's Degree in Psychology and Sociology from the University of Puerto Rico and completed some doctoral work in Education and Comparative Religion at New York University. In 1982, I traveled to Cuba, India, China and Japan to studio art, literature and cultural history, and then started photography with Jan Jurasek and attend the School of Visual Arts and the Maine Photographic Workshop.

My 85th birth was in 1964 in Corona Queens, as Victor Abel Donatello Vazquez (my friends called me Abel), where I gained fame in the streets as a graffiti writer by the moniker of Kool Angel Duster (a.k.a. KOOL A.D.), rackin cans, bombing the 7 trains, smokin dust, drinking 40's, fuckin pussy, bussin heads open until the age of 22 where I met my untimely death in a street brawl.

My 86th birth was in 1987 in Barcelona, Catalan, as Victor Vazquez Solsona. Having a natural talent at futbol,

I joined the Barcelona Futbol Club's youth team at age 11, moved up the ranks and joined the adult B-team when I turned 18. After 3 relatively uneventful years on my hometown team I was traded to Club Brugge over in Brussels, Belgium, where I saw much better luck for the next four years before being traded again, this time to Cruz Azul over in Hidalgo, Mexico. They barely played me at all that year and I was traded the next year to Toronto Futbol Club where I saw more action and continue to play at the time of the writing of this book.

My 442th self was born in 1893, as Frederick McKinnley Jones, but that's neither here nor there…My 87th birth was in 1989 in the town of Poio in the Providence of Pontevedra in Spain, as Victor Vazquez Rosales. Like my 86th self, I had a natural talent for futbol and the Celta de Vigo youth team before making the B-team when I turned 18. I saw little action and was traded on loan a year and a half later to Portonovo for a half season before returning to Celta for another uneventful year. I took the next year off and then joined Racing Ferrol over in Coruña, where I finally caught my stride and remain today at the writing of this book.My 88th self was born in San Francisco in 1983 as Victor Thomas Sterling Vazquez.

My 89th self was born in 1988 as Mohammad X in Paradise City.

My 90th self, Fausto Fausto, was born in 2014 in El Cerrito.

My 92nd self, Prince Existenz, was born in 1992 in Hunter's Boint.

My 93rd self was born in 2005 in Istanbul as Santa Sevgi, famed saint and Tennis Champion.

My 91st self, Johnny Baja was born in Alameda in the year 2222.

And so on and so forth…

Anyway, where was I?

Oh yeah…

I blinked my eyes and became Fausto Fausto.

I blinked again and the story was again in the third person.

Fausto Fausto blinked again, and chapter 78 disappeared.

79. AYYY

Fausto Fausto and Fausto Fausto were sitting side by side in a double black '77 Cadillac Double Happiness Amityville Special.

"How'd you like Chapter 78."

"Trash."

"Yeah, I thought so too."

They sat there for a while.

The radio was on. Some old Teng "Tina Tiger" Li-Chun song. A pretty ballad.

"Eh whatever, it was OK."

"Huh?"

"Chapter 78 was OK."

"Who cares?"

They drove to the End of the World, copped beers, sipped those.

The beers became clouds, the clouds became suns, pure light, energy.

The sky became water, the water became diamonds.

The diamonds, icelike, froze lakes into slick pavements, froze pavements into slick easements, froze easements into thick assessments, natural, the question of actuality, language, found and unfound sincerities, power steering, four wheel drive, the ceaseless filibustering of the scattering winds, dry leaf carci, empty November hazes, mind mending, the inky thinkinesses, the clouds of odd curiosity, the tyranny of the intellects, the thundering brows birthing new conundrums, furrowings, hustling breath, electric zap light stabbings, ghost elbows, the breakdancing nite movers, nice movers, the moonlite love makers, moon lovers, goony balloon rubbers, quadruple black truth metallic, ghetto nihilisms in unison, abandoning all previous tensions, time, the ever-approaching, poetic syncretic forensic, the words slick, the book-laffs, fluffy cloud books, atli, finger-traced, hyper-meta-geographical, indexia, papelly, papally regal, the grains, the slush, the wheat, the hefty slices, papyrus reeds, the ink of the poison frog, the puffer fish, the squid, hot mud in the sun, a cornflake in an English garden, a million billion trillion watts, a pow wow, feathery, the thunder drums, the horse hair swishing the dusty earth carpet, dreams made real, atomic paint peels, the skin stubs, the hot waters of the earth, magmic, faults of the crust, the fizzing states of matter, where does it all end, when, why, how, etc.

80. DISCO INFERNO

Fausto was playing dominoes with Carlos Serpiente at Chucho's new bar Cielo Rojo in Gitano Mojado in the Land of the Dead.

Chucho was playing KOOL A.D.'s beautiful mixtape AZTEC YOGA.

A joint called DISCO INFERNO was on, it was fire flames fuego, hella bars.

"Ay my fault for blasting you," said Fausto, "I was always taught to shoot first, ask questions later."

"I respect that."

"Here's your 7777 Bufalo Bufalo Xiuhcoatldtico Jan-Jeldo back."

"Eh, keep it."

"Thanks."

"No prob."

"Zany pistola."

"Very."

"Hey listen, I got a favor to ask you."

He slipped an envelope across the table. Carlos opened the envelope. It contained a beautiful field of flowers. Carlos stepped into the envelope and wandered through the field of flowers, met a beautiful woman there, her skin a deep black blue.

"You're beautiful," he said to the beautiful woman.

"I know," said the beautiful woman.

"What's your name?"

"時間の耐え難いほど遅い経過"

"That's a beautiful name."

"I know."

They stared at each other for 33 hours, frozen, statues of love.

They turned into water and the water turned into glass, the glass turned into light and the light turned into wind, the wind blew and that was the origin of music.

Carlos Serpientico and 時間の耐え難いほど遅い経過 went into business, selling their muted concepts of still, statuesque love in small vials, the junkies sucked the love air and got high.

Carlos Serpientico and 時間の耐え難いほど遅い経過 got married and forever did they do they thang, til def did they part.

Carlos Serpientico and 時間の耐え難いほど遅い経過 combined into one object, a tall clock tower, chiming the name, number, time, and aspect of every reason under the sun to be happy at any given second of the day, gibbering sick musical languages into the cold, stupid air of society, slooping swaggadaisical, trip trap brasilia, the wandering winds of timespace, the wondering sands of space-time, La Magia de la Yoga Azteca.

81. GENERIC PARTY FREESTYLE

Chuck Freight was throwing a big ass party at his brand new multi-million dead dollar Dead Beverly Hills mansion out in the Land of the Dead. He had just hit a major lick and he was celebrating. Everybody was there and they were all on full turn up, it was live. DJ You & DJ Me was on the ones and twos, spinning the hit KOOL A.D. song "GENER-IC PARTY FREESTYLE" off his recent mixtape AZTEC YOGA. The song was mindblowingly good. People were wilding the fuck out, they couldn't believe their ears.

Fausto, Mariposita, Chuck and Candi were posted up beneath some palms in a jacuzzi, drinking champagne.

A heard of zebras clopped by.

"Quite the lituation, no?" said Fausto to Mariposita.

"Quite," said Mariposita.

"Something of a rager," said Candi.

"Indeed," said Chuck

"Your house is crazy, Chuck," said Fausto.

"Yeah, its beautiful," said Mariposita.

"Thanks, yeah this fucker's huge, I love it."

"How many swimming pools again?"

"Can't remember."

"That's what's up."

"When's the opera start?"

Chuck had hired the Jing De National Theatre Troupe to perform the famed Payking Opera, DISQUE PARLANT BOHEME, at midnight.

"Midnight."

"I heard the lead actress in that troupe is an infamous tranny."

"Who, Xun-Xun? Yeah, very infamous."

"Isn't tranny a slur?"

"No, he self identifies as a tranny, specifically an 'infamous tranny,' I read it in an interview."

"Don't you mean she self-identifies as a tranny?"

"No, he said in the same interview that he doesn't care what pronoun people use."

"So why did you pick he?"

"I don't know, who cares?"

"I heard she is the richest living Payking Opera singer in the world."

"I heard she was the second richest, after Daddy Chang Yanqi."

"I heard the two were involved."

"Well, Daddy Chang Yanqi is in this opera too."

"You don't say?"

"Yup."

"Yeah, DISQUE PARLANT BOHEME is supposed to be on the short list for Greatest Story Ever told."

"I'm juiced to see it."

"The music is beautiful, it's my favorite opera, you guys are in for a real treat."

As the clock struck midnight, they found themselves seated in the garden amphitheatre, the curtains opening to a lavishly decorated Quingchan Dynasty style set. Daddy Chang Yanqi & Xun-Xun walked out on stage to enormous applause, sat at a table set with a Zong Dynasty vase holding two deep red Plum Blossoms, set with two Zong Dynasty ceramic plates each holding a triangular slice of blue watermelon.

They ate their watermelon slices in unison, bursting into twin blue flames and then twin blue mushroom clouds of blood, the scene evaporating into first a deep red blue, then a deep blue red, then a deep purple, then a deep white, then a deep, pure black, the swirling heat of la magic de la YOGA AZTECA.

82. TROPICAL TIME

Fausto and Mariposita were back in Novo Wimbo, in the exact same palm-thatched-roof-hut style cabin they stayed in last time overlooking the same beautiful black sand beach on the South Westernly Novo Ndoto coastline, overlooking The Pax Kusini Ocean, twixt the tropics of Scorpio Scorpio Allah and Dubiaku Hexachord.

They were zooted off a local flower known as Ndoto Nutmeg-Hazel Blossom, watching the waves perambulate, the churning desire perpetua de la Pax Kusini, the ceaseless, unyielding breathing of the waters.

They lay in the sun for 66 days, swam for 77 days, had butterfly relations for 88 days, slept for 99 days, woke up and repeated this cycle 99 times.

Time, the glacial lightning bolt, time, a funny circle, winding and whirling into itself, an expanding sphere, a twisting nautilus, a cloud cracking jokes, laughing at its own mirror reflection, time, cruel joker, laffer, the funny thing, time, tropical time.

The breeze blew through palm leaves, the water kissed and massaged the sand, stretching out, yawning.

The beach, the tropical beach of the Pax Kusini, twixt the tropics of Scorpio Scorpio Allah and Dubiaku Hexachord, a trill, benevolent latitude.

They conversed, relaxed, brimming with vivid, visceral joyous pulp organic bubbling from their echo boxes:

"THE REAL!"

"THE IMAGINED!"

"JOY, CRAZED JOY!"

"HIGHLY LIKELY!"

"MANIC SPLENDOR!"

"A FIERCE, NEUROTIC ECSTASY!"

"VIOLENT, POSITIVE!"

"THE SCREAMING FLOWERS OF THE BEAUTY ETERNAL!"

"THE SUN! AND THE MOON!"

"THE GUN AND THE GOON!"

"THE FLAMING CHARIOTS!"

"HELL AND HEAVEN!"

"HEAVEN AND HELL!"

"FREEDOM IS A NECESSITY!"

"MAY THE SUN SET FOREVER ON THE FACE OF EVIL!"

"LA MAGIA!"

"LA MAGIA!"

"LA YOGA AZTECA!"

"LA YOGA AZTECA!"

"THE AZTEC YOGA!"

"THE AZTEC YOGA!"

83. TRAP BRASILIA

Fausto traveled to Trap Brasilia on some business, rolled through the favelas in a 2020 Joop Terena 4 x 4 x 4 X 4, a clique of revolutionary tigres, badmen, shottas, etc. whipping along with him, an imposing motorcade.

They made it out the city proper and out into Campo Trappao, where an Italian style hunting cottage was parked in the shade of some Jacarandas. They pulled up in there for a little Bruncho dei Capi dei Capi, Pasta Craccatoni, ruby eye salad, white wine from the Decodificado Region.

The conversation was meta-philosophical in nature, with a greenish blue aura:

"The soft echo of hailstone against glass…"

"The sad brevity of the human experience…"

"An authentic sadness…"

"Roses, violets, tulips…"

"The juices of the known and the unknown…"

"To err fantastic…"

"The poetics of distrust…"

"A general theory of relative iniquity…"

"The sauce of language…"

"Barbary…"

"The true nature of wit…"

"Collections of emotions flying against each other…"

"Experience is the only history…"

"Why does the bird sing?"

"Why does the bird die?"

"Why does the bird fly?"

"The metallic teeth of truth chew the sky through the window…"

"A feeling is a funny thought…"

"There are no feelings…"

"There is nothing…"

"Niente…"

"Nada…"

"Nada…"

"Nichts…"

"沒有…"

"▨▨ ▨▨…"

"▨▨ ▨▨…"

"Rien…"

"Hakuna…"

"I kekahi mea…"

"Nada…"

"Nada…"

"Niente…"

"Niente…"

"Nothing…"

"Il corvo vola sopra la collina…"

"La volpe attraversa i boschi…"

"A caballo vamos al monte…"

"A cavalo nós vamos à floresta…"

"O tempo é um círculo, uma piada engraçada…"

"A verdade é um vento insignificante…"

"We come from dust and to dust we shall return…"

"Truth is dust, fantastic…"

"The waters of love shower the tree of peace…"

"Every inch of the earth is naked and vulnerable…"

"There is no hiding from the sun and its army of circumstance…"

"The eventual…"

"All light and all darkness meet within the sphere of time…"

"There is no knowing without being…""THERE IS NO BEING WITHOUT LOVING!"

"To know, to love, to be…"

84. GUNSHOTS IN THE DANCEHALL

"Guns lack the body of human truths," said Yogi Zero to Fausto and Chuck.

They were in the VIP section of a new club called The Immortal Dove in Dead Beverly Hills, enjoying some bottle service. Chuck knew the owner.

The sound system was large and beautiful, very powerful and effective, the speakers caused perfect vibrations within the fleshy tissues of the body.

The song was a KOOL A.D. number off his AZ-

TEC YOGA album. It was called GUNSHOTS IN THE DANCEHALL.

Fausto's 7777 Bufalo Bufalo Xiuhcoatldtico Jan-Jeldo came alive, jumped out of its holster and flew to the dance floor, started breakdancing.

The gun was amazing, acrobatic, athletic, manic, crazed, wild-eyed, firing toxic ideology bullets in every direction, the ideologies transmuted and refigured themselves, refracting and yin-yang boomeranging into prismatic, crystalline paragons of optimism, sprouting peace flowers from the air, it was a scene of heartrending transformation, transcendence, hope, positivity…

The 7777 Bufalo Bufalo Xiuhcoatldtico Jan-Jeldo exploded into a blue black mushroom cloud of blood in the shape of girl. The girl was the universal night, her stars kissed the eyes of the revelers, the party was everything, total peace, complete transcendence, Zero Death Infinity, El Amor Perpetual, La Magia, La Yoga Azteca, the ecstatic violence of peace, 10 ten million spinning Aztec Yogi, Sufis of the Realm, whirlin' dervishi, lyrical armed robbery of the soul's hate house, the sun-brilliant, moon-brilliant everlovin' nada, sloop fantasia, hyperlexia ridiculum, the flames magnetic, the springing life, tender vines squiddy ceremonial non-lingua limbgistical limbristical Allah Dada, a desperate, urgent thirst for peace, a gasping, lungs hugging air, sucking the sweet lifejoy, the summersaulting gnosi, dulcet, mellifluous, trumpeting sweet angelic euphony, rock sugar candy dissolving into an existential tea water, boiling, cosmic, pure light, pure black darkness, the everything nothing, the nothing every thing, singing the Peyote Karaoke, La Magia de la Yoga Azteca.

85. PRINCE OF PERSIA

Fausto was out in Shiraz feeling like the Prince of Persia.

He was at a little tea house perched on a river with Mariposita and his mother Khadijah X.

It was the first time Mariposita and Khadijah X had met and they were getting along.

"Back when I lived in Shiraz," said Khadijah X, "My name was Shirazi. I was a spiritualist and world-builder by occupation. I, in fact, created Shiraz, using highly potent meditation techniques that I taught Fausto's father when I met him and also Fausto himself. He's mostly squandered his spiritual capabilities on gambling. The apple doesn't fall far from the tree I suppose, but whatever, everything is everything."

"True, true.""But enough about me, tell me something about yourself, Mariposa.""There's nothing much to tell, I'm the most beautiful butterfly in the world.""You can say that again.""I'm the most beautiful butterfly in the world."

The tea was delicious, they all sipped on it, gazing at the rushing river waters, watching pink and blue dolphins leap out into the air and back under the flowing currents again.

The dolphins sang a beautiful song, one that could be heard even when they were under water, but was much clearer when they leapt out of the water, the constant leaping making for a wobbly, hyper-stereo, multi-phonic, oscillating orchestral net effect.

The dolphin song (sung in Dolphinian) loosely translated thusly:

O THE JOYWE RAVE ALLAHGOD IS AN EMPTY SYMBOLEMPTINESS IS FULL OF ITSELFTRUTH IS A FULL EMPTINESSO THE JOYOOTHE JOYTHE JOYWE RAVEWE RAVEALLAHJAH JAHA ROSE BY ANY OTHER NAMESTILL SMELL SWEET LORDMY SWEET LORDKRISHNA KRISHNAALLAH SYNCRETICTHE WATER IS THE AIRTHE EARTH IS THE WATERRAVE UNTO THE JOY FANTASTICTHE

BIG FULL EMPTY GOD JOY OF THE SKYAND IT'S STRANGE AND NUMEROUS STARSO SIMPLE WORDS COULD NEVER EXPLAINTHE MYSTERIES OF THE HEART

Khadijah X, who was fluent in Dolphinian, explained the song to Fausto and Mariposita.

"What a beautiful song," said Mariposita. "It's the most beautiful song in the world," said Khadijah X.

86. STILL GOT 50 POUNDS OF WEED IN THE TRUNK

Fausto was whipping thru the Adirondacks of South Kensington, out joogulatin, his traptitude was at Beastmode Levels.

Just then, a piggo popped up in the rearview trying to flash and caterwaul him over to the side of the road.

Not today.

Fausto bounced on the devil, put the pedal to the floor. Piggo flipped on his siren.

Fausto finessed the corners, wove, basket-like, through the forking, creek-like escape routes of Paradise Hills, slipping like a fish from the claws of a clumsy bear, almost shook the fuzz off but a lil kid ran into skreet chasing his frisbee, Fausto swerved and skidded into a tree.

He whipped out his 7777 Bufalo Bufalo Xiuhcoatldtico Jan-Jeldo, still love-stoned from that one magical night at The Immortal Dove, fired toxic ideology bullets at the cerdo, the ideologies transmuting and refiguring themselves, refracting and yin-yang boomeranging into prismatic, crystalline paragons of optimism, sprouting peace flowers from the air, exploding into a blue black mushroom cloud of blood in the shape of girl, the universal night, her stars kissing the eyes of the eternal love spirit, total peace, complete transcendence, Zero Death Infinity, El Amor Perpetual, La Magia, La Yoga Azteca, the ecstatic violence of peace, ten million spinning Aztec Yogi, Sufis of the Realm, whirlin' dervishi, lyrical armed robbery of the soul's hate house, the sun-brilliant, moon-brilliant everlovin' nada, sloop fantasia, hyperlexia ridiculum, the flames magnetic, the springing life, tender vines squiddy ceremonial non-lingua limbgistical limbristical Allah Dada, a desperate, urgent thirst for peace, a gasping, lungs hugging air, sucking the sweet lifejoy, the summersaulting gnosi, dulcet, mellifluous, trumpeting sweet angelic euphony, rock sugar candy dissolving into an existential tea water, boiling, cosmic, pure light, pure black darkness, the everything nothing, the nothing every thing, singing the Peyote Karaoke, La Magia de la Yoga Azteca.

The cop quit his job, became a monk in the Church of the Lost and Forgotten, braided his horrific memories into a rope of hope, hung himself, woke up in hell, worked there as a data analyst, eventually reincarnated as quiet girl named Monique Silva who became a nun in the First Church of La Magia de la Yoga Azteca.

87. LOUIS ARMSTRONG SORRY HOUSE FREESTYLE

Jazz trumpeter Louis Armstrong and book publisher Spencer Madsen were in Pianos Bar in the Lower East Side of Manhattan.

"I want to put out your book."

"But I've been dead for years."

"Doesn't matter, death isn't real. Plus, posthumous books make a lot of money."

"If you say so."

"So what's the book about?"

"You didn't read it?"

"Nah, couldn't find the time, I'm a busy man."

"It's a Western."

"Great, I love those, they make shit tons of money."

"Yeah, that's what I was figuring."

"Smart man."

"I helped invent jazz, basically. I'm a genius."

"I'm very happy to be in business with you."

"Why is your publishing company called Sorry House."

"It's an apology for its own stupid name, hahahahaha!"

"HAHAHAHAHA!"

"HAHAHAHAHA!"

They wiped the tears from their eyes.

"That was a really dumb joke."

"I know."

"No, but for real, why is your publishing house called Sorry House?"

"I don't know man, first thing that popped into my head."

"Fair enough. Who else is on your roster?"

"Me, Mira Gonzalez, Bunny Rogers, Richard Chiem and MOHAMMAD X F.K.A. KOOL MAN A.K.A. Victor "KOOL A.D." Thomas Sterling Vazquez-Solsona-Rosales-Chinaski-Allah-Mohammad-Ali-JesuCri'to-Elegua-Obatala-Chango-Chongo-Shongo, AKA THE KOOL-AID MAN, AKA Fausto Fausto even, AKA Ludwig Rainier Maria Von Trilke, AKA Maestro Don Ricardo Rigatonni-Rodriguez-Madera-Von-Trilke De La Vazquez-Velazquez-Solsona-Rosales-Chinaski-Ben-Salad-Al-Assad-Wong (B.K.A. Lil Ricky) AKA Cornelius Cornwall Thornbottom AKA Cornelius None, AKA etc., etc…"

"So in other words, a bunch of nobodies…"

"Mira Gonzalez has a decent Twitter following."

"No doubt."

"So, you down?"

"Sure."

They shook hands, ordered another round.

When their drinks came, they clinked glasses.

"To PEYOTE KARAOKE."

"To PEYOTE KARAOKE."

88. DUBS JAZZ GAME TOO

Louis Armstrong and MOHAMMAD X F.K.A. KOOL MAN A.K.A. Victor "KOOL A.D." Thomas Sterling Vazquez-Sol-sona-Rosales-Chinaski-Allah-Mohammad-Ali-Jesu-Cri'to-Elegua-Obatala-Chango-Chongo-Shongo, AKA THE KOOL-AID MAN, AKA Fausto Fausto even, AKA Ludwig Rainier Maria Von Trilke, AKA Maestro Don Ricardo Rigatonni-Rodriguez-Madera-Von-Trilke De La Vazquez-Velazquez-Solsona-Rosales-Chinaski-Ben-Salad-Al-Assad-Wong (B.K.A. Lil Ricky) AKA Cornelius Cornwall Thornbottom AKA Cornelius None, AKA Yogi Zero etc., etc. were about to play a 1-on-1 game of b-ball for the rights to the name PEYOTE KARAOKE.

Their publisher, Spencer Madsen, having read neither of their books, and having really only skimmed a few books in his life, was not even aware that not only did the books share the same title, they were, coincidentally, the exact same book from cover to cover, a fact that was made known to him by somebody working at the printing press. Apparently a common accident in publishing, or so somebody once told Spencer, he never bothered to look up whether or not it was true.

Spencer, publishing genius that he was, decided to settle the gentlemen's disagreement between Louis and (let's just call him Rapper B for the moment) Rapper B by refereeing a 1-on-1 game of b-ball between his two authors.

The match was held at the Oracle Arena in Oakland and the ticket prices were high (breaking the stadiums previous record held by the Fausto v. Fausto boxing match), the proceeds split 33.3% amongst the SPLC, the ACLU and Planned Parenthood.

The rules were an interesting variation on the classic half-court 1-on-1 basketball rules, instead of trying to shoot the basketball into the net, both authors instead were to sit at a wooden table facing each other eating a slice of purple watermelon, exploding into twin mushroom clouds of purple blood, evaporating into a pure white and then a pure deep dark black.

The authors performed their rite, the buzzer rang, a tie.

They went into overtime, this time eating white slices of watermelon, another tie.

Double O.T., black watermelon, another tie.

Triple O.T., blue watermelon, another tie.

Quadruple O.T., red watermelon, another tie.

And so on and so forth, running through every possible color of the rainbow and even a few colors not included on the rainbow.

The basketball game went on for 999 billion years, until it was officially recorded as an unbreakable tie, both authors winning the rights to PEYOTE KARAOKE.

89. RETURN 2 THA OCEAN UV PEACE

Fausto returned to the Ocean of Peace, recorded his thoughts into his satellite video phone:

A smooth expanse of linguistic feeling, a mush, a mesh, a rough material, a flesh.

Two linguists writhe in the sun like twin tongues, dancing flames.

To pull a supple art from the blooming imagios meta-optical.

To yank the yoke of the snarling steed of need, lips gnarled into a sneer of fear.

Desire is suffering, a whimpering echoing fading into darkness.

Truth is a flat static sky, unburdened of care or contempt.

Jokes are pulled from the night sky like cotton from the bush.

Lies are spun to gold by enchanted fingers on machines koanical.

Fiction creates fact and vice versa, ipso facto, ad infinitum.

A whip cracks a back raw, a chain cuts at extremities.

The brutality of life asserts itself at every rhetorical turn.

The slow rock of the mama hip, the shush of the night child.

A lullaby is a call to war in the dream realm.

A peace interrupted is not peace.

Peace be not peace.

Life is war and war is hell.

Hell is a lie and the devil a cartoon hastily wrought by the hand of the creator.

No style is free, why would it be?

Freedom is a choice and a legend, a process and a suggestion.

Freedom is a sunny day, a moony night.

All love hangs in the sky, stars, infinity.

Language sucks, a gift, a curse, a cruel and funny joke.

Time is a circle, a globe, repetition is a form of change.

Education is pain and repetition, education is joy, invention, freedom.

Experience is everything.

Make room for neither regret nor self congratulation.

Simply forgive and ask forgiveness.

Go about your day like a funny bird, flying, pecking at seeds when bored.

Life is whatever, hang out.

Platitudes ring, nonchalant smoke, curious memory.

Search for truth, or whatever, don't.

The truth is out there and will find you.

Reference and dutiful homage are lonely pursuits, like anything else.

Life is a lonely pursuit, filled with rambunctious curve balls.

Reality recognizes itself.

Cantos, Cadillac Moon, etc.

I'm here in the Ocean uv Peace, sussing the poetics of the oxygen tank, the states of matter, the multivalent gravities of Existent Peace and its legion faces...

La Magia, La Yoga Azteca…

90. THE DEVOTED

Dr. Goose Goose got pinched with a boatload of bricks and sang, ratting both Autua Jr. and Fausto Fausto.

Fausto Fausto was awaiting another execution our Gitano Mojado.

They provided a Meta-Catholic Priest to administer to Fausto Fausto his last rites and Final Sacred Mysterio Meta-Reconciliation.

Fausto sat in the confession booth and when the little window door slide open, he saw on the other side, the face of Fidel Castro.

Fidel: "¿Cual es el mejor equipaje de beisbol en el entero mundo?"

Fausto: "Tecnicalmente, Los Gigantes, pero espiritualmente Los Athleticos."

Fidel: "?Cual es el mejor equipaje de baloncesto en el entero mundo?"

Fausto: "Un empate entre Los Guerreros y Los Toros."

Fidel: "?Cual es el mejor equipaje de futbol en el entero mundo?"

Fausto: "Regular o Americano?"

Fidel: "Los dos."

Fausto: "Americano es un otro empate entre Los Cuarenta-Nueveros y Los Asaltantes, regular es un empate entre Brazil y Mexico."

Fidel: "?Quien es el mejor boxero en el entero mundo?"

Fausto: "Un empate de cinco vias entre Jack Johnson, Muhammad Ali, Teofilo Stevenson, Fausto Fausto y Fausto Fausto."

FIdel: "Cerran tus ojos."

Fausto closed his eyes.

Fidel: "Ahora, abrelos."

He opened them and saw that the Meta-Catholic Priest was not Fidel Castro, but in fact his father Mohammad X.

Mohammad X: "?Cual es el nombre del viento?"

Fausto: "Fausto Fausto."

The Meta-Catholic Final Sacred Mysterio Meta-Reconciliation dissolved and Fausto found himself walking right into his own execution, the white watermelon of death drowning him in the watermelon sugar, the fictive residues, sugars and shugars, caen and otherwise, La Magia Dulce de la Fruta de la Yoga Azteca, the mushroom cloud of black blood, dissolving into a colorless film, a hazy window framing an eternal nothing.

91. RAP JESUS (DUM SHINY)

Fausto Fausto awoke in the Land of the Double Dead, hanging from nails off a big pine cross, spitting hot fire flame bars, true fuego, rapping his natural born ass off, fountains of pure sun fire, Dum Shiny, the Sun Cat calling shoots, his little cat goons sniping at the snap of a claw, the Megasonic Meta-Fantastic Christblood Spraying like orca faucets in the Splash Zone, the shine ultimate, Hessian, Siddharthic, Magic, Mountainous, Monk-like, moonish, soonish, the dunes of the Orient, the dunes of Indiana, Eddie Said saying what he said, sipping the Kool-Aid on the Eid, idlewild, elderberry wine country, multiple Californias, Soak Zones, the churches of zex, tubular, orgiastic butterfly monsoons, pine salt, watermelon sugar, las blancas sabanas, a caravan, coin chests in tow, a steel metropolis on the move, in permanent flow, wandering, a moving city, a nomadic municipal skeleton, the bylaws rattled off, the accountants soaping the ink from their dismal fingers, total jazz and nothing else, the dummest, shiniest one, the coin tossed in the fountain, a dum wish, a dum shiny wish, shining in the glass hallways of heaven, the Sun Cat grinning his fire grin, rare confetti gunshots fired from hesitated lips, mayoral, celebrated as hot necessary metal, the unending slop cosmological, the various paper bag entrance exams for the escape pod, battleship earth, starship potempkin, the roguish children of multiple conflicting revolutions, the cranking of the gear shaft, friction of opposing forces, the grease of time, the shred teeth of the shark eidolon pixarical, out-swimming the bong ripping cornfed white gold holder, televisionary liescapes rendered in hell-blood inks, hot with furious intention, furious joy, the joy of the mark, gazing at one's own hand in shock and sweet, stunned awe, the hot white hand of the creationary creature, Dum Shiny.

Dr. Goose Goose, now running a trailer meth lab out in the deserts beyond Dead Fire City in the Land of the Dead, had become something of an amateur Pac Eidolon Kaleidoscope Soothseer.

He would spend hours gazing into the Pac Eidolon Kaleidoscope,, basking in the warm white milk of its lightglow. His posture got pretty bad, hunched, manic, twisted, gnarly, his eyes wide with a permanent far away fright.

He began to gather the loose strings of the Coincidental Poetics of the Particular and had fashioned himself a mighty large ball of string, which he planned to deliver to the large cat who held up the sun in the the Land of the Dead.

The cat's name was Sun Cat, he was feared, loved, and/ or respected by all.

On the 9th night of the final rotation of Saturn's Return to the Land of the Dead, Dr. Goose Goose rolled his Giant Ball of the Loose Strings of the Coincidental Poetics of the Particular over to the Sun Cat, who purred with appreciation for the offering and whispered a secret into Dr. Goose Goose's ear: "Snitches get stitches."

Dr. Goose Goose was popped in the head twice with a silenced Cafecito 888 by one of Sun Cats little cat shooters. The Sun Cat Family didn't play, except occasionally with balls of yarn.

The event was televised, Dr. Goose Goose's death. He televised it himself through the goggles of the Caen Shugar-soaked Pac Eidolon Kaleidoscope.

The television was infinite. A telescoping interior hallway, zooming into the centralized peace of the light bit, the screaming pixel, the zero, the line between zero and one, the one, La Magia Eternal de La Yoga Azteca, fountains of pure sun fire, dum shiny radiator water hissing from the steam engine of the Mozart Monster Truck, the hiss, the spitting fire flames, the crackle and cackle, the light, La Magia Dum Shiny.

93. WAIT A MINUTE

Fausto and Mariposita were in the Land of Women whipping a double pink 7777 Ferrari La Ferrari Ferrari La La on 77-inch platinum-plated, Swarovski-diamond-studded rims.

The women fell from the sky like rain, hallelujah, the exalted temple dome cielo, la lluvia de mujeres.

Skin and light were major aspects in the Land of Women, truth and exactitude...

The Land of Women rained sunshine upward to the skies.

The Land of Women was one single giant woman, the size of the sky itself, raining more women from her tear ducts, in to rivers of singing, swimming women. women flowers sprouted from woman soil, big leafy green women, little delicate women, tough curling vine women.

They stopped at a woman station, filled the La-La's gas tank up with the dreams of women.

They seared across the asphalt, deep black, paved by the souls of a thousand beautiful women.

The women were queens, kings, princesses, princes, nuns, monks, governesses, governors, duchesses, dukes, birds, butterflies, sirenas, unicorns, piratas, cats, dogs, tigers, leopards, panthers, zebras, snakes, clouds, raindrops...

The women painted light on the day and darkness on the night, cranked the wheel of time, sowed the seeds of love, sang the moon to sleep.

The women were wimin, wymyn, wimmin, girls even, grrrls, femmes, females, butches, dykes, bizexual, Sapphic lipstick Lesbos, azexual, gender queerz of all variety, the women had soft pink vaginas crying come, the women had beautiful hair of all textures, tight and loose curls, waves, long silky manes, big cottony naturals, long braids, short braids, ponytails, pigtails, bobs, buzz cuts, mohawks, tufts, bushes, bikini waxes, brazilians, pit hair, tattoos, full bosoms, small tetas, big booties, lil booties, slim doo doo makers stuffed inside pajamas, modest skin covered in fig-leaf, pieles desnudas sin verguenzas, light, darkness, truth, reason, wonder, shone pink, purple blue, white black, deep red, every yellow, the greens, every prismatic rainbow refraction of color, La Magia de la Yoga Azteca…

94. WHERE DO WE GO FROM HERE

Fausto and Mariposa were at a gathering of various guerilla tigres of the Forgotten Works of Los Discos…

"The grotesque fascism of yester-reality rears again its foul and ugly head!"

"Evil never dies, it only learns."

"Evil dies every second of its existence."

"Evil is death itself."

"Evil is dead."

"Death is nothing."

"Nothing is anything."

"Everything is anything."

"Everything is everything."

"Order! Order!"

"Chaos! Chaos!"

"No man is king, no woman queen."

"Truth; radiant, elusive…"

"Las hijitas de Ximena necesitan pañales…"

"Toma, quinientos pesos."

"Gracias."

"The solar panels will be repaired on Tuesday…"

"There is a leak in the southern wing mess hall kitchen sink."

"Jose said he's on it tomorrow morning."

"Tomorrow we ride on GitMo!"

"Mashalloah!"

"Alhumdulillah!"

"Allah Hu Akbar!"

"FREE EVERYBODY!"

"Elegua, Chango, Huitzilopochtli!"

"Jah Power Provide!"

"War pon de downpressa!"

"They'll eat the bread of sorrow!"

"The revolutionary spirit burns bright, never to extinguish!"

"My knife is my child, my rifle is my husband!"

"Peace is the truest reality forever!"

"Overstand the Power of Peace!"

They screamed platitudes all night, smoking red fern, chewing meta-menthe leaves, basing crystal from their rifles. As the Sun Cat held the sun up to the morning sky, Los Tigers rode to Giano Mojado. Mowed down the guards, freed the slaves.

"Another victory!"

"Victory is perpetual, inevitable!"

"Evil dies a thousand deaths per second!"

"Death is nothing!"

"La Magia!"

"Aztec Yoga!"

95. ROMEO Y JULIETA

Fausto and Mariposa were at the Teatro Municipal de Santo Oduduwa watching Romeo y Julieta.

The part of Julieta was played by Xochiquetzal Amorosa, the village bombshell and acting prodigy destined for larger fame abroad.

The part of Romeo was played by young heroe de futbol, centrocampista ofensivo Raul Nassor Menes, half Indio half Egyptian, son of a famous mathematician.

JULIETA: Romeo, Romeo, ?donde estas?

ROMEO: Aka.

JULIETA: Oh, no te vi.

ROMEO: Sta bien, k pasa

JULIETA: Nada…

ROMEO: ?Quieres cojer?

JULIETA: Por k no…

They fucked for hours on stage, running through every position, sweating, screaming with ecstasy. It was a very avant garde play.

At the end, they bowed, soaked with sweat and come, the audience roared with pure joyous love.

Fausto and Mariposita left the play scratching their heads.

"That's not how I remembered that play going."

"That's the beauty of Billy Cake Spear, never the same thing twice."

"Guess so."

"Billy's a real poet."

"No, I am."

"I was talking about you, Billy."

"Well, you pronounced my name wrong."

"There is no right or wrong."

"I can neither confirm nor deny that statement."

"No statement can ever be confirmed or denied."

"What does 'fake deep' mean?"

"Nothing."

"What is nothing."

"Anything."

"Everything is deep."

"The future's so heavy, baby, cause it's always gonna happen."

"Groovy as a ten cent movie."

"Twenny-Three Skidoo, funny face."

"I feel like Billy Cake Spear."

"You is, honey, you is."

"What is the most generous aspect of truth?"

"Its patience."

"What's the big idea?"

"The sum of all little ideas…"

"Where do you go when you reach the end?"

"Backwards."

96. PIANO MANE

Fausto strapped on his Virtual Realities Helmet and played a rousing bout of Be Anybody You Want To Be.

He chose to be famed hard moon bop pianist Cornelius None.

He played Ludwig Rainier Maria Von Trilke's Trillepathy for Several Seasons, the Devil's Repose in the Angel's Desert Campground; Sonata in Q Diagonal Majorus-Metti-Minorus, Third through Three Hundred-and-Thirty-Third movements, Adante Allegroza, Bellisima, weaved it together with the Cloud Atlas Sextet, and affixed those with watermelon sugar glue to Teng "Tina Tiger" Li-Chun's Number One Mega Hit, "The Moon Is The Metaphorical Language Of My Heart," throwing in a mash up of War and The Slang Wars by Temple Millenia and throwing in his own improvisations, slathering the melodic winds with Aztec Yogic riddims, counter-riddims, algo-riddims, et zetera.

The song was 999 billion years long, it went platinum 999 Trillion times, It had 999 Zillion plays, made 999 Scrillion dollars.

He whipped around in his black 9999 Cadillaca Buffalo Moon Daughter on 99 inch black gold rims, white wall tires, Martian leather rag top, listening to his 999 billion year song, t was long but beautiful, not a single note could've been cut, it was all crucial, unendingly compelling work, it demanded a long, thorough, dedicated listen.

He drove up to the Land of Women, Down to the Land of the Dead, over to the Forgotten Works, all over Los Discos, Las Angelas, Nueva Mexica, Gitano Mojado, etc. He did his funky lil thing.

Mariposita materialized on his shoulder, they blinked their eyes and were in an Isolation Chamber having mushroom cloud blood butterfly sex, they woke up on the beach of the Pax Kusini in Novo Ndoto, they fell asleep on the jet black moon, they swagged through Dreamland immaculate, humming hymnals of long dead shiny ghosts, cranking the singing jewel boxes of fate and patient energy, listened to the tinkly melodies…

97. SUBTLE CHANGES

They dug like dogs for complex emotions, found some, supped like hyenas at the carcass, they yelped for joy, dogs of love, they were war dogs, hungry, prowling, growling, gruff, utterly terrific, snapping their snow white shark teeth at the hissing air of freedom, they ran, the dogs, they ran, Fausto and Mariposita, two dogs, love dogs, war dogs, dogs in love, dogs at war, running through the night, the dog night, the foggy fog of the doggy dog night fogged vision and reason, clouded the senses with their own obtuse actualities, these dogs barked, these puppies yipped, they clamped onto the ankle of death and bought it to the ground, a gentle dragon kite, dropped by a tired wind, the sledder's whip cracking air, the trippy dog love, saliva dripping and dropping from their howling mouths, they dug, the dogs, for truth, funny lil feelings, new stuff, old stuff, bones, the skeletons of peace, truth, love, beauty, freedom, two free dogs, chewing on freedom bones, free flesh on free bones, free electricity brimming from their gray gummy dog brains, the dogs barked bright light, dum shiny, radiated, the dogs, the dogs, shining bright, dog stars burning in the night, Fausto and Mariposita, Romeo y Julieta, two doggies in the night, wet noses sniffing for the absolute pure now of love, La Magia de la Yoga Azteca, the ever-resplendent rainbow, crystalline pristine, aromatic, chirping like birds of precious gemstone, glowing opalescent in the exoskeletal sea, truth intelligent, the dog intelligence immaculate, the dog lick, the dog tongue, tongues of war and love, tongues wet with revolution, slick with the inimitable wet saliva of liberation, the slobber of ecstatic possibilities, the twin dogs galloped in union, tandem jet plane dogs, zipping and zooming rocketlike through the night, two running dogs, strong dogs, running fast.

98. NO SWEAT

They walked through the Desert of the Valley of Death, the dry heat evaporating the sweat from their skin, their organs cooking like soup in a clay oven, slowing turning into pure sun fire light…

The hot was so hot it was cold, the cold was so cold it burned a bright dark white black.

The stories had come and went, spoke from the infinity lips of some metallic creature, runed and tuned, an instrument of musical love and war.

The communes inflated and deflated with the ebbs, flows, eddies and tides of the righteous and the weak.

The souls were celebrated, washed, wrung dry, thrown in the air like pizza dough.

Evil lay dead, oozing milk white blood.

The buzz, the hum electric, the light bulbs burning fires electrical in a dark permanent night.

It was an easy day, they ambled this way and that, peaked into caves and crevices, climbed trees, gazed at clouds and then stars…

They jumped in a river and swam to the sea. They saw what they could see. They sat on a seesaw. They sawed the seesaw into two seats and sat. They seasoned their heads with hats. They peopled their pens with cats of the sun, sold Sun Cat Milk for pretty pennies.

Language fell away beneath hem, useless.

They carved names and songs in 100 trees, the trees whispered secrets to each other and held hands.

There was nothing to do and nothing not to do.

There was everything in front of them, they jumped, landed in everything. They jumped up into everything and lived there a while, taking everything in. Everything jumped into them and they jumped with everything up into the big wonderful everything.

There was no denying their dum stupid love, shiny with funky fire.

There was no denying the ice cold facts, the dead white evil there on the flat pavement. The hot black peace, the never-ending love moving through the waters of forever.

They lay in bed feeling The Joy, The Whole Joy and Nothing But the Joy.

The Joy filled them and they filled The Joy.

The Joy killed them and from that death The Joy again to them gave birth.

They spake of The Joy thusly:

"The Joy."

"The Joy."

"The Joy!"

"The Joy!"

"THE JOY!"

"THE JOY!"

THE JOY!

THE JOY

The Joy forever, beyond language, grammar, punctuation, etc.

The Pure Plain Joy.

The Forever Always Infinity Joy, The Joy Infinite…

They rolled around in The Joy and The Joy, in turn, rolled around in them.

They held The Joy up to the light and examined it. Yup, pure 100% Joy.

The Joy was so high you couldn't get over it, so low you couldn't get under it, so wide you couldn't get around it.

The only thing they could do was be inside of The Joy, be The Joy, let The Joy be them.

The Joy, The Joy, The Joy…

The Joy.

THE JOY.

The Big Great Joy.

The Joy, The Wonderful Joy.

The Joy Stupendous.

The Stupid Dum Shiny Joy.

The Joy, Whatever.
Cheap, chill Joy.
Trill Joy, Treal Joy, True & Real Joy.
The Joy Splendid, The Joy Ridiculous...
The Joy Forever, The Never Not Joy...
The Sleepy Joy, The Mellow Joy...
The Joy Radiant, The Joy Fantastic....
The Joy of Joys, The Joy Beyond Joys...
The Nervous, Jittery Joy...
The Joy Bubbling up from The Spring of Joy.
The Springing, Sproinging Joy.
The Joy, Forked, Venomous, Serpentine.
The Joy, Sweet, Soft, Dulcet, Cooperative.
The Groovy Stupid Joy.
The Crazy Joy.
The Joy, Spiritual.
The Pure Soul Joy.
They felt it.
The Joy.
They felt The Joy.
The Joy.
The Joy.
THE JOY.
THE JOY
THE JOY
THE JOY
THE JOY
THE JOY
THE JOY

100. ALONE IN SAN FRANCISCO

Fausto was walking alone in San Francisco, down Mission,

headed south, through Bernal Heights, Excelsior, Ingleside, Oceanview, Crocker Amazon, down over to the Cow Palace, the site of the infamous Skirmish of the Liberated Replicants he'd read about in the Fake News, he kept walking til he hit Santo Francotico, and then Santa Francesca,..

He whistled as he walked, a jazz tune, a brilliant, vivacious melody, brand new in the world, truly beautiful.

He breathed in the tranquil solitude, the city breathing its lights into his skull, inhabiting his flesh, sitting like gold dust on his brain matter.

He came to an electric blue piano, and played the sweet melody in his head.

The melody went up and down and side to side, it breathed in and breathed out, breathed in, breathed out,

breathed in, breathed out, breathed in, breathed out,
breathed in, breathed out, breathed in, breathed out,
breathed in, breathed out, breathed in, breathed out,
breathed in, breathed out, breathed in, breathed out,
breathed in, breathed out, breathed in, breathed out,
breathed in, breathed out, breathed in, breathed out,
breathed in, breathed out, breathed in, breathed out,
breathed in, breathed out, breathed in, breathed out,
breathed in, breathed out, breathed in, breathed out,
breathed in, breathed out, breathed in, breathed out,
breathed in, breathed out, breathed in, breathed out,
breathed in, breathed out, breathed in, breathed out,
breathed in, breathed out, breathed in, breathed out,
breathed in, breathed out, breathed in, breathed out,
breathed in, breathed out, breathed in, breathed out,
breathed in, breathed out, breathed in, breathed out,
breathed in, breathed out, breathed in, breathed out,
breathed in, breathed out, breathed in, breathed out,
breathed in, breathed out, breathed in, breathed out,
breathed in, breathed out, breathed in, breathed out,
breathed in, breathed out, breathed in, breathed out,
breathed in, breathed out, breathed in, breathed out,
breathed in, breathed out, breathed in, breathed out,
breathed in, breathed out, breathed in, breathed out,
breathed in, breathed out, breathed in, breathed out,
breathed in, breathed out, breathed in, breathed out,
breathed in, breathed out, breathed in, breathed out,
breathed in, breathed out, breathed in, breathed out,
breathed in, breathed out, breathed in, breathed out,
breathed in, breathed out, breathed in, breathed out,
breathed in, breathed out, breathed in, breathed out,
breathed in, breathed out, breathed in, breathed out,
breathed in, breathed out, breathed in, breathed out,
breathed in, breathed out, breathed in, breathed out,
breathed in, breathed out, breathed in, breathed out,
breathed in, breathed out, breathed in, breathed out,

breathed in, breathed out, breathed in, breathed out,
breathed in, breathed out, breathed in, breathed out,
breathed in, breathed out, breathed in, breathed out,
breathed in, breathed out, breathed in, breathed out,
breathed in, breathed out, breathed in, breathed out,
breathed in, breathed out, breathed in, breathed out,
breathed in, breathed out, breathed in, breathed out,
breathed in, breathed out, breathed in, breathed out,
breathed in, breathed out, breathed in, breathed out,
breathed in, breathed out, breathed in, breathed out,
breathed in, breathed out, breathed in, breathed out,
breathed in, breathed out, breathed in, breathed out,
breathed in, breathed out, breathed in, breathed out,
breathed in, breathed out, breathed in, breathed out,
breathed in, breathed out, breathed in, breathed out,
breathed in, breathed out, breathed in, breathed out,
breathed in, breathed out, breathed in, breathed out,
breathed in, breathed out, breathed in, breathed out,
breathed in, breathed out, breathed in, breathed out,
breathed in, breathed out, breathed in, breathed out,
breathed in, breathed out, breathed in, breathed out,
breathed in, breathed out, breathed in, breathed out,
breathed in, breathed out, breathed in, breathed out,
breathed in, breathed out, breathed in, breathed out,
breathed in, breathed out, breathed in, breathed out,
breathed in, breathed out, breathed in, breathed out,
breathed in, breathed out, breathed in, breathed out,
breathed in, breathed out, breathed in, breathed out,
breathed in, breathed out, breathed in, breathed out,
breathed in, breathed out, breathed in, breathed out,
breathed in, breathed out, breathed in, breathed out,
breathed in, breathed out, breathed in, breathed out,
breathed in, breathed out, breathed in, breathed out,
breathed in, breathed out, breathed in, breathed out,
breathed in, breathed out, breathed in, breathed out,

breathed in, breathed out, breathed in, breathed out,
breathed in, breathed out, breathed in, breathed out,
breathed in, breathed out, breathed in, breathed out,
breathed in, breathed out, breathed in, breathed out,
breathed in, breathed out, breathed in, breathed out,
breathed in, breathed out, breathed in, breathed out,
breathed in, breathed out, breathed in, breathed out,
breathed in, breathed out, breathed in, breathed out,
breathed in, breathed out, breathed in, breathed out,
breathed in, breathed out, breathed in, breathed out,
breathed in, breathed out, breathed in, breathed out,
breathed in, breathed out, breathed in, breathed out,
breathed in, breathed out, breathed in, breathed out,
breathed in, breathed out, breathed in, breathed out,
breathed in, breathed out, breathed in, breathed out,
breathed in, breathed out, breathed in, breathed out,
breathed in, breathed out, breathed in, breathed out,
breathed in, breathed out, breathed in, breathed out,
breathed in, breathed out, breathed in, breathed out,
breathed in, breathed out, breathed in, breathed out,
breathed in, breathed out, breathed in, breathed out,
breathed in, breathed out, breathed in, breathed out,
breathed in, breathed out, breathed in, breathed out,
breathed in, breathed out, breathed in, breathed out,
breathed in, breathed out, breathed in, breathed out,
breathed in, breathed out, breathed in, breathed out,
breathed in, breathed out, breathed in, breathed out,
breathed in, breathed out, breathed in, breathed out,
breathed in, breathed out, breathed in, breathed out,
breathed in, breathed out, breathed in, breathed out,
breathed in, breathed out, breathed in, breathed out,
breathed in, breathed out, breathed in, breathed out,
breathed in, breathed out, breathed in, breathed out,
breathed in, breathed out, breathed in, breathed out,
breathed in, breathed out, breathed in, breathed out,
breathed in, breathed out, breathed in, breathed out,

breathed in, breathed out, breathed in, breathed out,
breathed in, breathed out, breathed in, breathed out,
breathed in, breathed out, breathed in, breathed out,
breathed in, breathed out, breathed in, breathed out,
breathed in, breathed out, breathed in, breathed out,
breathed in, breathed out, breathed in, breathed out,
breathed in, breathed out, breathed in, breathed out,
breathed in, breathed out, breathed in, breathed out,
breathed in, breathed out, breathed in, breathed out,
breathed in, breathed out, breathed in, breathed out,
breathed in, breathed out, breathed in, breathed out,
breathed in, breathed out, breathed in, breathed out,
breathed in, breathed out, breathed in, breathed out,
breathed in, breathed out, breathed in, breathed out,
breathed in, breathed out, breathed in, breathed out,
breathed in, breathed out, breathed in, breathed out,
breathed in, breathed out, breathed in, breathed out,
breathed in, breathed out, breathed in, breathed out,
breathed in, breathed out, breathed in, breathed out,
breathed in, breathed out, breathed in, breathed out,
breathed in, breathed out, breathed in, breathed out,
breathed in, breathed out, breathed in, breathed out,
breathed in, breathed out, breathed in, breathed out,
breathed in, breathed out, breathed in, breathed out,
breathed in, breathed out, breathed in, breathed out,
breathed in, breathed out, breathed in, breathed out,
breathed in, breathed out, breathed in, breathed out,
breathed in, breathed out, breathed in, breathed out,
breathed in, breathed out, breathed in, breathed out,
breathed in, breathed out, breathed in, breathed out,
breathed in, breathed out, breathed in, breathed out,
breathed in, breathed out, breathed in, breathed out,
breathed in, breathed out, breathed in, breathed out,
breathed in, breathed out, breathed in, breathed out,

breathed in, breathed out, breathed in, breathed out,
breathed in, breathed out, breathed in, breathed out,
breathed in, breathed out, breathed in, breathed out,
breathed in, breathed out, breathed in, breathed out,
breathed in, breathed out, breathed in, breathed out,
breathed in, breathed out, breathed in, breathed out,
breathed in, breathed out, breathed in, breathed out,
breathed in, breathed out, breathed in, breathed out,
breathed in, breathed out, breathed in, breathed out,
breathed in, breathed out, breathed in, breathed out,
breathed in, breathed out, breathed in, breathed out,
breathed in, breathed out, breathed in, breathed out,
breathed in, breathed out, breathed in, breathed out,
breathed in, breathed out, breathed in, breathed out,
breathed in, breathed out, breathed in, breathed out,
breathed in, breathed out, breathed in, breathed out,
breathed in, breathed out, breathed in, breathed out,
breathed in, breathed out, breathed in, breathed out,
breathed in, breathed out, breathed in, breathed out,
breathed in, breathed out, breathed in, breathed out,
breathed in, breathed out, breathed in, breathed out,
breathed in, breathed out, breathed in, breathed out,
breathed in, breathed out, breathed in, breathed out,
breathed in, breathed out, breathed in, breathed out,
breathed in, breathed out, breathed in, breathed out,
breathed in, breathed out, breathed in, breathed out,
breathed in, breathed out, breathed in, breathed out,
breathed in, breathed out, breathed in, breathed out,
breathed in, breathed out, breathed in, breathed out,
breathed in, breathed out, breathed in, breathed out,
breathed in, breathed out, breathed in, breathed out,
breathed in, breathed out, breathed in, breathed out,
breathed in, breathed out, breathed in, breathed out,
breathed in, breathed out, breathed in, breathed out,
breathed in, breathed out, breathed in, breathed out,

breathed in, breathed out, breathed in, breathed out,
breathed in, breathed out, breathed in, breathed out,
breathed in, breathed out, breathed in, breathed out,
breathed in, breathed out, breathed in, breathed out, etc.,
etc., etc., etc., etc., etc., etc., etc., etc., etc., etc., etc., etc.,
etc., etc., etc., etc., etc., etc., etc., etc., etc., etc., etc., etc.,
etc., etc., etc., etc., etc., etc., etc., etc., etc., etc., etc., etc.,
etc., etc., etc., etc., etc., etc., etc., etc., etc., etc., etc., etc.,
etc., etc., etc., etc., etc., etc., etc., etc., etc., etc., etc., etc.,
etc., etc., etc., etc., etc., etc., etc., etc., etc., etc., etc., etc.,
etc., etc., etc., etc., etc., etc., etc., etc., etc., etc., etc., etc.,
etc., etc., etc., etc., etc., etc., etc., etc., etc., etc., etc., etc.,
etc., etc., etc., etc., etc., etc., etc., etc., etc., etc., etc., etc.,
etc., etc., etc., etc., etc., etc., etc., etc., etc., etc., etc., etc.,
etc., etc., etc., etc., etc., etc., etc., etc., etc., etc., etc., etc.,
etc., etc., etc., etc., etc., etc., etc., etc., etc., etc., etc., etc.,
etc., etc., etc., etc., etc., etc., etc., etc., etc., etc., etc., etc.,
etc., etc., etc., etc., etc., etc., etc., etc., etc., etc., etc., etc.,
etc., etc., etc., etc., etc., etc., etc., etc., etc., etc., etc., etc.,
etc., etc., etc., etc., etc., etc., etc., etc., etc., etc., etc., etc.,
etc., etc., etc., etc., etc., etc., etc., etc., etc., etc., etc., etc.,
etc., etc., etc., etc., etc., etc., etc., etc., etc., etc., etc., etc.,
etc., etc., etc., etc., etc., etc., etc., etc., etc., etc., etc., etc.,
etc., etc., etc., etc., etc., etc., etc., etc., etc., etc., etc., etc.,
etc., etc., etc., etc., etc., etc., etc., etc., etc., etc., etc., etc.,
etc., etc., etc., etc., etc., etc., etc., etc., etc., etc., etc., etc.,
etc., etc., etc., etc., etc., etc., etc., etc., etc., etc., etc., etc.,
etc., etc., etc., etc., etc., etc., etc., etc., etc., etc., etc., etc.,
etc., etc., etc., etc., etc., etc., etc., etc., etc., etc., etc., etc.,
etc., etc., etc., etc., etc., etc., etc., etc., etc., etc., etc., etc.,
etc., etc., etc., etc., etc., etc., etc., etc., etc., etc., etc., etc.,
etc., etc., etc., etc., etc., etc., etc., etc., etc., etc., etc., etc.,
etc., etc., etc., etc., etc., etc., etc., etc., etc., etc., etc., etc.,
etc., etc., etc., etc., etc., etc., etc., etc., etc., etc., etc., etc.,

etc., etc., etc., etc., etc., etc., etc., etc., etc., etc., etc., etc.,
etc., etc., etc., etc., etc., etc., etc., etc., etc., etc., etc., etc.,
etc., etc., etc., etc., etc., etc., etc., etc., etc., etc., etc., etc.,
etc., etc., etc., etc., etc., etc., etc., etc., etc., etc., etc., etc.,
etc., etc., etc., etc., etc., etc., etc., etc., etc., etc., etc., etc.,
etc., etc., etc., etc., etc., etc., etc., etc., etc., etc., etc., etc.,
etc., etc., etc., etc., etc., etc., etc., etc., etc., etc., etc., etc.,
etc., etc., etc., etc., etc., etc., etc., etc., etc., etc., etc., etc.,
etc., etc., etc., etc., etc., etc., etc., etc., etc., etc., etc., etc.,
etc., etc., etc., etc., etc., etc., etc., etc., etc., etc., etc., etc.,
etc., etc., etc., etc., etc., etc., etc., etc., etc., etc., etc., etc.,
etc., etc., etc., etc., etc., etc., etc., etc., etc., etc., etc., etc.,
etc., etc., etc., etc., etc., etc., etc., etc., etc., etc., etc., etc.,
etc., etc., etc., etc., etc., etc., etc., etc., etc., etc., etc., etc.,
etc., etc., etc., etc., etc., etc., etc., etc., etc., etc., etc., etc.,
etc., etc., etc., etc., etc., etc., etc., etc., etc., etc., etc., etc.,
etc., etc., etc., etc., etc., etc., etc., etc., etc., etc., etc., etc.,
etc., etc., etc., etc., etc., etc., etc., etc., etc., etc., etc., etc.,
etc., etc., etc., etc., etc., etc., etc., etc., etc., etc., etc., etc.,
etc., etc., etc., etc., etc., etc., etc., etc., etc., etc., etc., etc.,
etc., etc., etc., etc., etc., etc., etc., etc., etc., etc., etc., etc.,
etc., etc., etc., etc., etc., etc., etc., etc., etc., etc., etc., etc.,
etc., etc., etc., etc., etc., etc., etc., etc., etc., etc., etc., etc.,
etc., etc., etc., etc., etc., etc., etc., etc., etc., etc., etc., etc.,
etc., etc., etc., etc., etc., etc., etc., etc., etc., etc., etc., etc.,
etc., etc., etc., etc., etc., etc., etc., etc., etc., etc., etc., etc.,
etc., etc., etc., etc., etc., etc., etc., etc., etc., etc., etc., etc.,
etc., etc., etc., etc., etc., etc., etc., etc., etc., etc., etc., etc.,
etc., etc., etc., etc., etc., etc., etc., etc., etc., etc., etc., etc.,
etc., etc., etc., etc., etc., etc., etc., etc., etc., etc., etc., etc.,
etc., etc., etc., etc., etc., etc., etc., etc., etc., etc., etc., etc.,
etc., etc., etc., etc., etc., etc., etc., etc., etc., etc., etc., etc.,
etc., etc., etc., etc., etc., etc., etc., etc., etc., etc., etc., etc.,
etc., etc., etc., etc., etc., etc., etc., etc., etc., etc., etc., etc.,

etc., etc., etc., etc., etc., etc., etc., etc., etc., etc., etc., etc.,
etc., etc., etc., etc., etc., etc., etc., etc., etc., etc., etc., etc.,
etc., etc., etc., etc., etc., etc., etc., etc., etc., etc., etc., etc.,
etc., etc., etc., etc., etc., etc., etc., etc., etc., etc., etc., etc.,
etc., etc., etc., etc., etc., etc., etc., etc., etc., etc., etc., etc.,
etc., etc., etc., etc., etc., etc., etc., etc., etc., etc., etc., etc.,
etc., etc., etc., etc., etc., etc., etc., etc., etc., etc., etc., etc.,
etc., etc., etc., etc., etc., etc., etc., etc., etc., etc., etc., etc.,
etc., etc., etc., etc., etc., etc., etc., etc., etc., etc., etc., etc.,
etc., etc., etc., etc., etc., etc., etc., etc., etc., etc., etc., etc.,
etc., etc., etc., etc., etc., etc., etc., etc., etc., etc., etc., etc.,
etc., etc., etc., etc., etc., etc., etc., etc., etc., etc., etc., etc.,
etc., etc., etc., etc., etc., etc., etc., etc., etc., etc., etc., etc.,
etc., etc., etc., etc., etc., etc., etc., etc., etc., etc., etc., etc.,
etc., etc., etc., etc., etc., etc., etc., etc., etc., etc., etc., etc.,
etc., etc., etc., etc., etc., etc., etc., etc., etc., etc., etc., etc.,
etc., etc., etc., etc., etc., etc., etc., etc., etc., etc., etc., etc.,
etc., etc., etc., etc., etc., etc., etc., etc., etc., etc., etc., etc.,
etc., etc., etc., etc., etc., etc., etc., etc., etc., etc., etc., etc.,
etc., etc., etc., etc., etc., etc., etc., etc., etc., etc., etc., etc.,
etc., etc., etc., etc., etc., etc., etc., etc., etc., etc., etc., etc.,
etc., etc., etc., etc., etc., etc., etc., etc., etc., etc., etc., etc.,
etc., etc., etc., etc., etc., etc., etc., etc., etc., etc., etc., etc.,
etc., etc., etc., etc., etc., etc., etc., etc., etc., etc., etc., etc.,
etc., etc., etc., etc., etc., etc., etc., etc., etc., etc., etc., etc.,
etc., etc., etc., etc., etc., etc., etc., etc., etc., etc., etc., etc.,
etc., etc., etc., etc., etc., etc., etc., etc., etc., etc., etc., etc.,
etc., etc., etc., etc., etc., etc., etc., etc., etc., etc., etc., etc.,
etc., etc., etc., etc., etc., etc., etc., etc., etc., etc., etc., etc.,
etc., etc., etc., etc., etc., etc., etc., etc., etc., etc., etc., etc.,
etc., etc., etc., etc., etc., etc., etc., etc., etc., etc., etc., etc.,
etc., etc., etc., etc., etc., etc., etc., etc., etc., etc., etc., etc.,
etc., etc., etc., etc., etc., etc., etc., etc., etc., etc., etc., etc.,
etc., etc., etc., etc., etc., etc., etc., etc., etc., etc., etc., etc.,

etc., etc., etc., etc., etc., etc., etc., etc., etc., etc., etc., etc.,
etc., etc., etc., etc., etc., etc., etc., etc., etc., etc., etc., etc.,
etc., etc., etc., etc., etc., etc., etc., etc., etc., etc., etc., etc.,
etc., etc., etc., etc., etc., etc., etc., etc., etc., etc., etc., etc.,
etc., etc., etc., etc., etc., etc., etc., etc., etc., etc., etc., etc.,
etc., etc., etc., etc., etc., etc., etc., etc., etc., etc., etc., etc.,
etc., etc., etc., etc., etc., etc., etc., etc., etc., etc., etc., etc.,
etc., etc., etc., etc., etc., etc., etc., etc., etc., etc., etc., etc.,
etc., etc., etc., etc., etc., etc., etc., etc., etc., etc., etc., etc.,
etc., etc., etc., etc., etc., etc., etc., etc., etc., etc., etc., etc.,
etc., etc., etc., etc., etc., etc., etc., etc., etc., etc., etc., etc.,
etc., etc., etc., etc., etc., etc., etc., etc., etc., etc., etc., etc.,
etc., etc., etc., etc., etc., etc., etc., etc., etc., etc., etc., etc.,
etc., etc., etc., etc., etc., etc., etc., etc., etc., etc., etc., etc.,
etc., etc., etc., etc., etc., etc., etc., etc., etc., etc., etc., etc.,
etc., etc., etc., etc., etc., etc., etc., etc., etc., etc., etc., etc.,
etc., etc., etc., etc., etc., etc., etc., etc., etc., etc., etc., etc.,
etc., etc., etc., etc., etc., etc., etc., etc., etc., etc., etc., etc.,
etc., etc., etc., etc., etc., etc., etc., etc., etc., etc., etc., etc.,
etc., etc., etc., etc., etc., etc., etc., etc., etc., etc., etc., etc.,
etc., etc., etc., etc., etc., etc., etc., etc., etc., etc., etc., etc.,
etc., etc., etc., etc., etc., etc., etc., etc., etc., etc., etc., etc.,
etc., etc., etc., etc., etc., etc., etc., etc., etc., etc., etc., etc.,
etc., etc., etc., etc., etc., etc., etc., etc., etc., etc., etc., etc.,
etc., etc., etc., etc., etc., etc., etc., etc., etc., etc., etc., etc.,
etc., etc., etc., etc., etc., etc., etc., etc., etc., etc., etc., etc.,
etc., etc., etc., etc., etc., etc., etc., etc., etc., etc., etc., etc.,
etc., etc., etc., etc., etc., etc., etc., etc., etc., etc., etc., etc.,
etc., etc., etc., etc., etc., etc., etc., etc., etc., etc., etc., etc.,
etc., etc., etc., etc., etc., etc., etc., etc., etc., etc., etc., etc.,
etc., etc., etc., etc., etc., etc., etc., etc., etc., etc., etc., etc.,
etc., etc., etc., etc., etc., etc., etc., etc., etc., etc., etc., etc.,
etc., etc., etc., etc., etc., etc., etc., etc., etc., etc., etc., etc.,
etc., etc., etc., etc., etc., etc., etc., etc., etc., etc., etc., etc.,
etc., etc., etc., etc., etc., etc., etc., etc., etc., etc., etc., etc.,

etc., etc., etc., etc., etc., etc., etc., etc., etc., etc., etc., etc.,
etc., etc., etc., etc., etc., etc., etc., etc., etc., etc., etc., etc.,
etc., etc., etc., etc., etc., etc., etc., etc., etc., etc., etc., etc.,
etc., etc., etc., etc., etc., etc., etc., etc., etc., etc., etc., etc.,
etc., etc., etc., etc., etc., etc., etc., etc., etc., etc., etc., etc.,
etc., etc., etc., etc., etc., etc., etc., etc., etc., etc., etc., etc.,
etc., etc., etc., etc., etc., etc., etc., etc., etc., etc., etc., etc.,
etc., etc., etc., etc., etc., etc., etc., etc., etc., etc., etc., etc.,
etc., etc., etc., etc., etc., etc., etc., etc., etc., etc., etc., etc.,
etc., etc., etc., etc., etc., etc., etc., etc., etc., etc., etc., etc.,
etc., etc., etc., etc., etc., etc., etc., etc., etc., etc., etc., etc.,
etc., etc., etc., etc., etc., etc., etc., etc., etc., etc., etc., etc.,
etc., etc., etc., etc., etc., etc., etc., etc., etc., etc., etc., etc.,
etc., etc., etc., etc., etc., etc., etc., etc., etc., etc., etc., etc.,
etc., etc., etc., etc., etc., etc., etc., etc., etc., etc., etc., etc.,
etc., etc., etc., etc., etc., etc., etc., etc., etc., etc., etc., etc.,
etc., etc., etc., etc., etc., etc., etc., etc., etc., etc., etc., etc.,
etc., etc., etc., etc., etc., etc., etc., etc., etc., etc., etc., etc.,
etc., etc., etc., etc., etc., etc., etc., etc., etc., etc., etc., etc.,
etc., etc., etc., etc., etc., etc., etc., etc., etc., etc., etc., etc.,
etc., etc., etc., etc., etc., etc., etc., etc., etc., etc., etc., etc.,
etc., etc., etc., etc., etc., etc., etc., etc., etc., etc., etc., etc.,
etc., etc., etc...

And as the final note hung in the air, Mariposita landed on his shoulder.

"Nice song," she said, "What do you call it?"

"El Cerrito Natural."

Made in the USA
Middletown, DE
18 March 2022